"I thought you'd only go to bed for love."

Laurier's harsh words prompted Alex to tell him the truth. "I would. I do love you. But not enough to sacrifice my work," she said. "I can't give that up any more than you can give up yours. It's not fair to ask me."

"Was it fair to let me fall in love with you, knowing you had no intention of becoming my wife?"

"I didn't know you were in danger of loving me," Alex murmured sadly. "I had no way of knowing it would hurt you when we parted."

"I should think the fact that I didn't try to rush you into bed should have indicated that my interest was more than casual," Laurier responded bitterly. "And if you want a man in your bed tonight, try the bar downstairs!"

ANNE WEALE is one of Harlequin's busiest writers—and also one of the most traveled. She gave up her original career as a journalist to follow her husband to the Far East. British citizens by birth, Anne and her husband have lived for the past five years in a Spanish villa high above the Mediterranean. They have traveled extensively, researching new romantic backgrounds—New England, Florida, the Caribbean, Italy, and their latest journeys have taken them through Canada to Australia and the Pacific. Swimming, interior decorating, antique hunting and needlepoint are among Anne's many interests.

Books by Anne Weale

ANTIGUA KISS
FLORA
SUMMER'S AWAKENING

HARLEQUIN PRESENTS

HARLEQUIN ROMANCE

Don't miss any of our special offers. Write to us at the following address for information on our newest releases.

Harlequin Reader Service
901 Fuhrmann Blvd., P.O. Box 1397, Buffalo, NY 14240
Canadian address: P.O. Box 603,
Fort Erie, Ont. L2A 5X3

ANNE WEALE

lost lagoon

Harlequin Books

TORONTO • NEW YORK • LONDON
AMSTERDAM • PARIS • SYDNEY • HAMBURG
STOCKHOLM • ATHENS • TOKYO • MILAN

At this point in history, when so many couples have two careers, the place they choose to settle in and whose work opportunities they pursue become serious new issues that must be negotiated. Two careers challenge the traditional structure of family life.

AMERICAN COUPLES: Money Work Sex
by Philip Blumstein PhD and Pepper Schwartz PhD

Harlequin Presents first edition June 1988
ISBN 0-373-11085-5

Original hardcover edition published in 1987
by Mills & Boon Limited

CHAPTER ONE

ALEXANDRA CLIFFORD had been in Vancouver for less than two weeks when she saw him for the first time.

Her arrival in western Canada had coincided with a period of Indian summer. Day after October day had been sunny and warm, although there was usually an autumnal nip in the air when, at seven a.m., she set out for her morning exercise on the sea wall walk around Stanley Park.

Her turning point was the Nine O'Clock Gun, an old naval muzzle-loaded cannon cast in England in 1816 and brought to British Columbia towards the end of that century.

At the gun Alex would pause for a moment, shading her eyes against the rising sun to look across the great harbour towards the Second Narrows Bridge and then at the mountains rising behind North Vancouver on the far shore.

Then she would turn on her heel and swing back the way she had come, a tall, long-legged young woman wearing white shorts and a T-shirt, her streaky blonde shoulder-length hair swinging in rhythm with her stride.

Most of the early morning exercisers who used the sea wall were joggers, predominantly male. Alex agreed with Victoria Principal's dictum that jogging wasn't good for breasts. Although her own bosom wasn't as large as the TV star's, she saw no reason to risk spoiling her smaller but well-shaped breasts by jogging every day. She preferred a modified form of Steve Reeves's power-walking; and she thought a lot of the older men who jogged past her, huffing and puffing, some of them barely able to gasp 'good morning', would be well advised to slow down.

Alex always said good morning to everyone she passed because, at that hour of the day, in that setting, it seemed the natural thing to do. Most people returned her greeting. One of the few exceptions had been a Japanese tourist who, perhaps on his way to the airport, had asked his taxi to stop where the scenic drive round the park ran close to a point on the sea wall where he could take some last photographs of the Downtown skyline of high-rise offices and apartment buildings lit by the early sun.

His reaction to Alex's greeting had been a nervous sideways glance and an incoherent mumble. Perhaps because she was a blonde he took her for one of Vancouver's exotic dancers and was afraid that, given any encouragement, she might try to pick him up. Probably respectable Japanese women didn't say good morning to strange men at any hour of the day.

Musing on cultural differences in behaviour, she strode on towards Hallelujah Point where, long ago, the Salvation Army had held meetings, their hallelujahs ringing across the water to the streets of a much smaller city than the one which now spread its suburbs almost as far as the American border.

On the morning that she first saw the tall man, she had turned around at the gun and was looking at the fluorescent red logo above the revolving restaurant on the forty-second floor of the Sheraton Hotel, when suddenly another shadow loomed beside her own on the left-hand side of the line which divided the path into sections for pedestrians and cyclists.

Although the cyclists made no sound, the heavy breathing of joggers and the pad of their feet on the asphalt usually announced their presence as they came up behind her.

But the tall black-haired man with his well-defined shoulder and back muscles, whose passing gave her a slight start, ran so silently that his footfalls had been inaudible against the diminishing drone of a float plane which had taken off from the harbour a few minutes earlier.

As the distance between them expanded, her gaze travelled down from the powerful back to the hard male backside inside the thin cotton running shorts. Then to the long strong legs which carried him over the ground with a light, easy, rhythmic lope which was beautiful to watch.

He had passed her too swiftly and unexpectedly for her to catch even a glimpse of his face, but from the rear he was the most impressive-looking man she had seen in a long time, if ever. Nature had endowed him with a tall, perfectly proportioned frame, and it was obvious from the way he ran that he kept his body in fine shape. Not an ounce of superfluous flab marred the tapering lines of his torso. White tennis socks emphasised the shapely swell of his calves. Above his knees, his tanned thighs were hard with muscle. His legs were not very hairy, but the hair on his head was as thick and glossy as the fur of the black squirrels which lived in the park, or the plumage of the north-western crows which frequented the sea wall. As he'd passed her, she had noticed that at his nape his hair was damp. Her nostrils had caught the faint, not unpleasant scent of fresh sweat.

She wondered how far he had run and why she hadn't seen him before. Perhaps he was only in Vancouver for a short time, staying at the Westin Bayshore, the expensive hotel on the southern shoreline of the harbour, close to the entrance to the park.

Between the gun and the point where she left the park, the sea wall followed serpentine curves. In places the path was shaded by the tall spruces which in the centre of the park formed a small but dense forest intersected by trails. The morning air carried the fragrance of the woods mingled with the tang of the ocean and, at low tide, the pungent aroma of exposed mud.

Long before she reached the Rowing Club building, the tall man had disappeared. It might be that he'd come to the park by car and now had driven away, either west along Georgia towards the business section of the city, or through the heart of the park to the famous Lion's Gate Bridge which spanned the First Narrows leading into the harbour.

From the underpass near the lake known as Lost Lagoon, Alex walked up Alberni, still keeping up her fast pace and still thinking about the tall runner and wondering if his face would have been a disappointment.

Exactly forty-five minutes after setting out, she took the lift up to her self-catering suite on the tenth floor of a hotel on Robson Street. By ten minutes to eight she was under the shower, shampooing her thick fair hair, her mind back on her work.

He passed her again the next morning.

As he drew swiftly ahead, she was conscious of being slightly piqued that he hadn't even said 'Hi!' as most younger men usually did.

Exactly how old he might be was difficult to judge from his rear view. With that superb physique he could be younger than she was, yet somehow she didn't think so. There was something about him, something she couldn't pin down, which suggested he was at least thirty.

She wondered if he had noticed her, or if he was too deep in thought to pay attention to any of the people he passed. Without being vain, Alex knew she had a good figure and legs which attracted appreciative glances from the opposite sex. If the tall man had not even glanced at her, it had to be for one of three reasons.

He was using his exercise time to do some concentrated thinking, as she herself often did.

He was married or otherwise committed, and he didn't have a roving eye.

He was homosexual.

In her first few days in Vancouver she had picked up a giveaway newspaper, the *West Ender*, from a stack inside the entrance to the city's central library which she had joined both for her work and her pleasure. The West End was the part of the city between Downtown and Stanley Park. It was clear from the paper's personal ads that the area had a large gay community. The personal column was full of lonelyhearts ads, mostly inserted by gay men in search of companionship, but with a sprinkling of appeals from heterosexual men and women.

One ad which had caught her eye ran:

> I need a very special kind of woman. Am cute, reasonably slim, male, 35, Caucasian. Need true, true love from one who would never leave me. She's gotta be creative, spiritual, sensitive and not expect me to be the only breadwinner. I'm not a professional man, just a working type in a bachelor pad.
>
> She's got to expect me only to photograph model aeroplanes till I'm a hundred and four and maybe write the odd jazz ballad or throw together some bizarre video humour. Who knows? I might create a hit and strike it rich, but most likely not. She must like grey skies as well as blue, and be the cook as well as me. Can we fit all this into a very long happy life?

Another ad had read:

> Good woman looking for that good man. I'm single, white, female, non-smoker (though not fanatically so), 36 (though I look much younger), 5′4½″, slim, fair-haired, not unattractive, intelligent, idealistic, inquisitive, sensitive, romantic, self-reliant. Interests include music, nature, cycling, swimming, quiet walks,

movies, cooking, science, philosophy, laughing and lots more. If you're intelligent, honest, generally open-minded, possess at least a smidge of innate curiosity, and are preferably no older than 40, why not reply to Box 4000, c/o *West Ender*.

One or two of the advertisements had made her lips curl with distaste. But the majority appeared to have been inserted by people genuinely in need of caring companionship.

Alex wondered if the tall runner who was now a hundred yards ahead of her, passing the gatekeeper's hut at the entrance of Deadman's Island, could be the man who had advertised:

New in town, 6 ft, good physique, career gentle-man. Considered quite attractive, intelligent. Caring with a good sense of humour. Seeks an attractive, sensual, occasional mistress (NO HOOKERS) for mutually satisfying affair of the heart, possible relationship. Send photo and requirements to Box 2500, *West Ender*.

The noisy honking of a small flock of Canada geese flying in from the direction of English Bay on the far side of the West End made Alex look up to watch them come in to land.

On her first walk in the park she had been surprised at how tame they were, allowing people to walk close to them. The shading of their plumage from black through dark beige to ivory was in line with her personal colour scheme. She had a small, expensive wardrobe of classic styles in neutral colours which allowed her, in a single suitcase, to carry clothes for every eventuality in every climate.

What kind of ad should I write if I needed to advertise for a man? she wondered, striding past the catwalk leading to the docks of the Royal Vancouver Yacht Club.

> Interior designer, aged 27, 5'6" tall, 125 lbs, natural blonde, grey eyes, neither pretty nor plain, too involved with her career to have time for marriage/ children, seeks unattached professional man with whom to share occasional evenings at the theatre, concerts, etc, and nights of enthusiastic but emotionally uninvolved lovemaking. Must be non-smoker. Looks less important than brains, sense of humour, good manners.

Would an ad on those lines make her sound unnatural or, worse, amoral? she wondered.

In fact by most people's standards her life had been almost puritanical. She had been quite old, twenty-two, before she had been to bed with anyone. Then she and her first lover had lived together for two years. Since then there had been no one; three years of nun-like chastity because most of the men of the right age were married and it was against her principles even to dine with a married man. Sometimes her work obliged her to have a business lunch with someone else's husband, but she made it a rule never to have dinner with one, even when she was reasonably confident he wanted nothing more than a table companion and someone to show the photographs of his family.

Alex's rules for life were many and various. They ranged from never taking pills other than vitamins to investing a proportion of her income and paying regular amounts into the bank account of the aunt who had raised her after her parents were killed.

Many of her rules were a reaction to the life she had led with Aunt Jo and her husband, Ben Fisher. The Fishers had

had six children of their own and had adopted two more, one black and one Asian, before the advent of their orphaned niece had increased their family to nine.

Nine children, two adults and Ben's ailing widowed mother packed into a five-bedroom house. From the time she had gone to live with them, Alex had never had a room of her own or clothes which hadn't been handed down from one of her cousins.

She had been well fed and enfolded with loving kindness. For that she would always be deeply grateful. But she had never had a minute's privacy and seldom a minute's peace, and that, to a little girl accustomed to living in a spacious apartment with two intellectual grown-ups who spent most of their leisure reading, playing chess and listening to classical music, had been a severe culture shock.

Alex had never really adjusted to living in the crowded, disorganised Fisher household where frequent vociferous arguments, people running up and down stairs, TV, at least one radio playing full blast and an elderly dishwasher rumbling almost non-stop to cope with thirty-six place settings a day had been the norm.

Nine years in the Fisher ménage had made her determined to achieve the luxuries of space and silence. And she had. Her life was now exactly the way she wanted it.

The only thing lacking was that, like the 'new in town' six-footer who had advertised for 'an occasional mistress', she sometimes needed a man to put strong arms round her and kiss her, and make her feel a desirable female as well as a successful careerist.

Thinking about it, she was sure the ad had not been put in by the tall runner. He looked more than six feet tall, and if his face matched his figure he wouldn't need to advertise. Women would fall over themselves to couple with that highly tuned athletic body.

Why am I thinking so much about sex at the moment?

she asked herself as she strode down the slope of the underpass beneath busy Highway 99 which was bringing suburban commuters into the centre and taking other motorists out to North and West Vancouver.

The answer, she knew, was that the strong force of nature was still trying to make her comply with the pattern laid down for the survival of the species. Biologically, women had only one purpose; to give birth to young and mother them.

Now, after centuries of subservience to that natural law, at last woman had other options. But their body chemistry still urged them to mate and most of them did. In the late teens and early twenties, a combination of chemistry and curiosity was almost irresistible.

Alex's resistance had been strengthened by what had happened to one of her cousins. Susan Fisher had found herself pregnant by a boy she had known all her life, a friend of her eldest brother. Her upbringing made it unthinkable to have an abortion and, although her mother and father would have helped her to be a single parent, she had felt obliged to accept the boy's offer to marry her. Both had been far too young and immature for a permanent relationship and had quickly fallen out of love.

Their experience had made the then sixteen-year-old Alex see 'falling in love' for what it really was—a trap for the unwary. One she was determined to sidestep.

Women had to face up to the fact that it was impossible to combine marriage with a career, especially a career which involved a great deal of travelling. In her observation, those who did attempt to combine the skills of the housewife with another job invariably ran themselves ragged.

Whatever Helen Gurley Brown might claim about 'having it all', the incontrovertible truth was that you couldn't have your cake and eat it. You had to make a choice. And she had opted for financial independence and the satisfaction of an absorbingly interesting job which brought her to places such as Vancouver, surely one of the world's most beautiful cities.

For three mornings in succession the tall man passed her, running like poetry in motion.

The next morning was a Sunday. Members of the Rowing Club were doing exercises on the large veranda outside the building as she passed. She was out later than usual because she hadn't gone to bed until the small hours. Not because she had spent Saturday night dining and dancing; she had spent the evening alone, working on the project which was the reason for her presence in Vancouver.

Walking back from the gun, she saw no sign of the runner. Perhaps he didn't run on Sundays, or perhaps he had been and gone. If he didn't live in Vancouver he might have finished his business there and left the city after his breakfast yesterday, or even late Friday night if he had a wife or girlfriend he was eager to get back to.

Curiosity about his face nagged her. Don't be silly, she told herself. He had beautiful muscles. He ran well. He may have been a total creep. Think about something else.

A black squirrel finished burying something in the grass and whisked up a tree, making her smile at its bright-eyed alert little face.

The leaves of the small sugar maples along the sea wall were beginning to turn red although, so she had been told, their change would not be as vivid as that of the maples on the eastern side of this vast country. Here in the west the climate was milder and wetter. The maple trees needed cold to make them put on their full brilliance.

She was nearing the gabled Rowing Club, built on pilings rising from the water—or the mud, according to the tidal flow—when a man appeared on the overhead ramp which connected the club with a road on a higher level than the path.

He was wearing an open-necked shirt and a tweed sports jacket. At first his head was turned away. Although his hair was neatly brushed, not ruffled as when he was running, she recognised the back of his head. Then he turned and glanced in her direction.

For the first time she saw his face and drew in her breath in a slight involuntary gasp.

He was about thirty-five, not handsome but very attractive. At the front the thick dark hair sprang from a broad high forehead above black brows and dark brown eyes. All his features were forcefully cut and superimposed with two deep lines down his cheeks which suggested a man who smiled easily.

He wasn't smiling at the moment. At the sight of her he had stopped and was looking down from the ramp with an oddly intent expression.

Was it possible he had been as curious about her face as she about his? No; in that case he would have glanced over his shoulder after running past her.

Unaware that her stride had shortened almost to a stroll, Alex lifted her face to meet the searching dark gaze bent upon her.

'Good morning,' she said, with less than her usual self-possession.

He inclined his head. 'Good morning.'

Then he moved on towards the road and she quickened her pace and hurried on towards the underpass. She was disturbed to find that her heart was pumping as rapidly as it did when she walked very fast up a steep hill.

On Monday morning, punctually at seven, she set out for her walk aware that if the tall man ran past her this morning without speaking it would be a disappointment and a blow to her self-esteem.

In the past twenty-four hours she had spent a good deal of time—far too much time—trying to judge from the two

words he had spoken whether he was a Canadian or, like
herself, a foreigner.

When she reached the gun a Seabus was crossing the
harbour. She stopped, ostensibly to watch it, but out of the
corner of her eye she was watching the stretch of sea wall
round the corner on which the gun stood, hoping to see a
lithe figure lope into view.

She lingered there for several minutes. Then, annoyed
with herself, she began the return walk.

He came by while she was passing the group of painted
Indian totem poles. At first she thought he was going to pass
without acknowledging her presence, but then he stopped
running and turned to face her.

He smiled, a warm friendly smile which fulfilled the
promise of the two grooves down his cheeks and showed her
some lesser crinkles at the corners of his eyes.

'Good morning. Mind if I walk with you?'

She shook her head, smiling back. 'Not at all. Isn't this
weather glorious?'

He nodded and fell into step with her. 'This is a good
time of year. My name is Laurier Tait, and you are . . .'

'Alexandra Clifford.'

'Miss, Mrs or Ms?'

'Miss,' Alex said firmly. She couldn't see the point of Ms.

'Are you here on vacation, Miss Clifford, or are you
living in Vancouver?'

'I'm here for eight weeks, of which I've already had two.
It's not a vacation. I'm working here.'

'You're from England, aren't you?'

'Yes, I am. Are you a Vancouverite?'

'Not really. My mother came from Quebec. My father's
forebears were Scots. I was born in Paris and I work in
Hawaii. I know Vancouver pretty well because I've been
coming here since I was a small boy. I'm staying with my
grandmother.'

So that was why he was so tanned.

She said, 'Hawaii sounds a fun place to work. What do you do there?'

'I'm an oceanographer. To be specific, a marine geologist.'

'Really? How interesting. You're the first one I've met.'

'Considering how much of the earth's surface is covered by water, there aren't many of us,' he said drily. 'It's a fairly new science. One of the fathers of oceanography was Benjamin Franklin, who published a map of the Gulf Stream way back in 1770. But modern oceanography didn't get going until this century.'

'What attracted you to it?'

'My pioneer blood, I guess. Now that all the land masses have been explored, the oceans are the last frontiers left on this planet. What's your line of work, Miss Clifford?'

'I'm designing the penthouse suites for the new Connaught Tower Hotel.'

'You must be a top-class designer to have snatched a commission like that from under the noses of the local talent.'

'I wouldn't say that, but I'm aiming in that direction.'

'You say you've been here two weeks. Have you been shown the view of the city from Cloud Nine at the Sheraton?'

'No, I haven't.'

'May I take you up there for a drink before dinner this evening?'

What she should have said, and she knew it, was, 'I'm afraid I'm tied up this evening.' And, if he suggested an alternative, have made some other pleasant excuse. She had had plenty of practice at politely declining invitations.

But although she knew it was unwise, she ignored the mental alarm bells. 'I'd like that very much.'

'Good. Where are you staying?'

She told him.

'I'll pick you up at six. It takes about an hour for the bar to revolve full circle. Right now between six and seven is the right time to see the city lighting up. See you at six.'

He broke into a run, leaving her full of excitement at the prospect of a date with him. And full of misgivings at starting something which might complicate her trouble-free existence.

Wrapped in a bath towel, Alex reviewed her wardrobe and decided on a black silk chemise and a softly gathered skirt which, together, looked like a dress. With a black cashmere jacket, her black Chanel slingbacks and a small black calf bag, she would look right wherever he took her.

Having chosen what to wear, she returned to the bathroom to use Rochas's *Mystère* deodorant, talc and toilet water. Her body still had a light tan from regular sunbathing on the little roof garden which went with her studio flat in London. For holidays she usually went to Italy before or after the main tourist season. She had been planning an October visit to Florence, but then this assignment in Vancouver had come up.

The hotel was an addition to a chain of luxury hotels all over North America. She had happened to meet the chairman of the company which owned them at a party given by an English actor who had a share in a restaurant she had designed. John Kassinopolis, the Toronto-based president of the Connaught Corporation, had been impressed by her work. He had asked her if she were interested in designing the four penthouse suites at the top of his newest hotel, and Alex had jumped at the opportunity. If she could make a resounding success of it, it would be sure to lead to other commissions in Canada and America. By the time she was thirty-five, she was determined to be among the top echelon of internationally known designers. Working for John Kassinopolis was a major step in that direction.

She had been ready for ten minutes when the telephone

rang and the desk clerk told her Mr Tait was in the lobby.
After a final glance at her reflection in the large mirror in
the living area of the suite, she picked up her key and set out
for her first taste of Vancouver's night life.

Laurier was looking at a display of tourist brochures
when she stepped out of the lift at street level. He was
wearing a grey suit with half an inch of pink shirt-cuff
showing below the edge of his jacket sleeves.

When she said, 'Hello', and he swung round, she saw that
his tie was pink with light and dark grey diagonal stripes.
His clothes struck exactly the right balance: conservative
but not boring. She felt men should take some interest in
their clothes, but not too much. Her trained eye recognised
the superlative quality of the cloth he had chosen and the
hallmarks of superior tailoring. She wouldn't have expected a scientist to be able to afford a bespoke suit of that
order. Perhaps he had private means in addition to his professional income.

'Hello.' He held out his hand.

As they shook hands, his dark eyes took in her shiny-
clean hair brushed back in what Americans called a 'status
pull', showing the twisted gold hoops in her ears to match
the rope chain round her neck.

She had made up her face with great subtlety so that, to a
masculine eye, she might seem to be wearing no make-up.
Actually it had taken twenty mintues to enhance the smoky
grey of her irises and highlight her cheekbones with the
careful use of gleamer and blusher.

Although she always took time to make the best of
herself, tonight as she used her cosmetics she had been
aware that her motive was not quite as simple as the wish to
look a woman whose impeccable style extended to every
aspect of her life. She had found herself wanting to look
beautiful and—without being blatant—sexy as well.

Even though it had dismayed her to be conscious of such
dangerous inclinations, she hadn't been able to stop herself

outlining and painting her mouth to emphasise rather than play down the curving fullness of her lips.

But his glance didn't linger on her mouth. After a swift scrutiny of her general appearance, he looked down at her feet.

'Are your shoes OK for walking as far as the Sheraton? It's only a couple of blocks.'

'Yes, I never wear shoes I can't walk in.' She turned her ankle to show him that the heels of her pumps only increased her height by two inches. Nothing could be less elegant, she felt, than the jerky ungraceful gait caused by stilt-like high heels.

He moved to the door and opened it for her. As they walked outside into the Robsonstrasse, the middle section of Robson where chic boutiques and speciality food shops gave the street a European atmosphere, Laurier said, 'I don't want to risk my licence so I left the car in the garage. There are pretty stiff penalties here for drinking and driving. It's wiser to take a taxi on special occasions.'

He looked down at her, smiling, a certain glint in his dark eyes which made her pulse quicken suddenly.

'Did you have far to come?' she asked.

'No, my grandmother lives near a bus route which comes along Granville Street.'

As they came to an intersection and waited for the raised hand sign to give place to the white 'walk' signal, he slipped his hand under her elbow.

Alex found it hard to relate his self-assured debonair manner and expensive clothes with a willingness to use public transport in preference to his own car. To most men their car was part of their macho image. None of them ever admitted to being less than a brilliant driver and few of them took the alcohol limit too seriously.

Misinterpreting her curious glance, he said, 'Don't worry, I'm not expecting you to walk everywhere tonight, We'll take a taxi to the restaurant.'

'Unless it's pouring with rain, I like walking,' she answered.

It crossed her mind that he might have lost his driving licence. He was, after all, a total stranger, a man who, basically, had picked her up. That they were both fitness enthusiasts didn't really constitute an introduction although she had persuaded herself that it did.

'So I've noticed,' he said, steering her across the street. 'What do you do for exercise when you can't take your early walk? In the winter, or when it's raining?'

'Then I walk in my lunch break or after the rain has stopped. It doesn't often rain all day.'

'It does in Vancouver,' he said drily. 'This is where Noah must have been when it rained forty days and nights. My God, can it rain here!'

'What about running in Hawaii? Is it too hot to run there?'

'It's not an ideal running climate because of the humidity. But it's OK first thing in the morning, before the sun's up. I get most of my exercise surfing. Have you ever tried it?'

She shook her head. 'I can swim, but not well. I've never lived near the sea ... or, as you say, the ocean.'

The Sheraton lobby was busy with travellers who had just arrived and others who were on their way out for the evening. During the few minutes they had to wait for a lift, she was aware of other women looking at her tall companion.

Well built six-footers were not uncommon in Vancouver, but Laurier Tait had something special about him. Even when fully dressed and standing still, he emanated an impression of physical strength and perfect co-ordination.

Her thoughts ran ahead to the end of their evening together. She wondered uneasily if the reason he had left his car at home was because he expected to be spending the night in town—with her.

As far as the thirtieth floor the lift was crowded; she was forced to stand with her shoulder and arm in contact with his chest. When some people got out, leaving room for the rest of the passengers to shift their positions, she was quick to make a space between him and herself.

He bent and said, close to her ear, 'You smell delicious.'

'Thank you.' She found herself blushing.

This is ridiculous, she thought, in confusion. I'm behaving like a seventeen-year-old. Pull yourself together, Alex.

Most of Cloud Nine was a restaurant but one segment of the ring-shaped area revolving round the central core containing the lifts was a lounge-bar. They were lucky. A table by the window was being vacated as they arrived.

'What would you like to drink, Alexandra?' Laurier asked, waiting for her to sit down before he took the chair on the opposite side of the round table. 'Gin and tonic? A spritzer?'

'May I have a glass of red wine, please?'

'I'll join you.' He gave the order to the waiter who was deftly removing the glasses and ashtray used by the previous occupants.

She wondered whether to tell him she was usually called Alex. Her parents had always used her full name but the Fishers had shortened it and, although the staff at her school had called her Alexandra, she had always been Alex to her contemporaries.

Hearing Laurier say Alexandra reminded her of her father who had also had a deep voice, although with a different accent from that of the man sitting opposite.

He was looking at the view and it should have had all her attention because, from the forty-second floor, they were looking down on the rest of the West End's high-rise buildings, with an eagle's view of the forest on the Stanley Park peninsula and a breathtaking panorama of the city's environs and the mountains.

However, at this moment she was more interested in the lines of his strongly marked profile. The high-bridged bony nose, the prominent slant of his cheekbones and the forceful jut of his chin which, allied to his black hair and deeply bronzed skin, combined to give him the looks that, before coming to Canada, she had associated with North American Indians.

Disappointingly, those descendants of the country's original inhabitants whom she had seen lounging about the streets of Vancouver had been poor examples of their race. Judging by what she had read in the newspapers, here as elsewhere in the world the arrival of settlers from other lands had meant the slow ruination of the indigenous population.

Forcing her gaze away from his compelling profile, she looked down from their high vantage point and saw that several of the lower buildings had trees and shrubs on their flat roofs.

The waiter returned with their wine and a bowl of miniature pretzels. When he had gone, Laurier lifted his glass and, leaning towards her, said, 'Here's to the fortunate chance of my time in Vancouver coinciding with yours.'

Politeness obliged her to smile and raise her own glass, but the toast carried implications which made her guiltily aware that she had no business to be with him. She was here in defiance of one of her most basic principles—not to get involved with a man again. Her relationship with Peter had been a mistake. She had emerged from the experience determined not to repeat the error.

Laurier said, 'How did you come to be a designer, Alexandra?'

'I suppose my career has its roots in the dolls' house my mother bought me for my ninth birthday. She and my father shared a passion for eighteenth-century porcelain. They spent a lot of their spare time looking for additions to their collection in antique shops, and I used to go with them. In those days—twenty years ago—you could still buy little things for dolls' houses quite cheaply. One of my first treasures was a miniature sewing machine which was actually a Victorian tape-measure. My parents thought it was an interest to encourage and after I'd collected quite a few little bits Mummy bought me a house to put them in.'

She paused, a little embarrassed at having let slip the childish name for her parent. But Elena Clifford had died when her daughter was ten. All Alex's memories of her were those of a pre-teens child whose loving relationship had not yet been complicated by the stresses and strains which sometimes came with adolescence.

'What kind of dolls' house was it?' Laurier asked.

'A Victorian suburban villa with a fancy porch and gingerbread bargeboards,' she told him. 'There are one or two old-fashioned houses on Alberni Street, and in other parts of the West End, which remind me of it.'

He said, 'It's not so long since the West End was full of houses like that. All this high-rise——' with a gesture at the buildings below them '—is a comparatively new phenomenon. I can remember this city when the tallest buildings were the Sun Tower down on West Pender, the Vancouver Hotel—the big railway Gothic building with the green roof—and the Marine Building with the art deco reliefs.'

She nodded. 'I know the one you mean. I haven't done the usual sightseeing round, the trip up Grouse Mountain and so on, but I have walked all round the Downtown area and admired the architectural marvels. There's a fascinating range of styles, from the Grecian temple Bank of Commerce to the greenhouse style of the new Law Courts and that marvellous cascading "river" in Robson Square,' she added enthusiastically.

Laurier snapped a pretzel with noticeably white and healthy teeth. 'It's hard to realise, seeing this huge spread of urban development, that only two hundred years ago this part of the continent was hardly known to the people colonising eastern Canada,' he said reflectively. 'Even after the gold rushes up in the Klondike and along the Fraser River, most of this area we're looking at had nothing but trappers' cabins and some logging camps and lumber mills.'

'What brought your forebears to Canada?' she asked.

'Bad behaviour,' he said, with a grin. 'My great-grandfather, who was born in Scotland, was sent packing by his father for some escapade. As a young man he was an explorer. Then he settled down here to become a farmer and trader. His son went into the liquor business. It's been said that whisky and the search for adventure and wealth created this city.'

'And your father?'

A slight frown contracted his eyebrows. 'My father inherited the liquor business and would have liked me to succeed him. Fortunately I have two half-brothers who don't share my lack of interest in balance sheets and management techniques. They're carrying on the business, leaving me free to do my thing. Have you been to see the Museum of Anthropology at UBC yet?'

She knew that the three initials were how most people referred to the University of British Columbia, and U Vic meant the University of Victoria in the provincial capital on Vancouver Island, a ferry-trip across the island-dotted Gulf of Georgia.

'No, I haven't, but it's on my list of things to see.'

'I'd like to take you,' he offered. 'I think you'd enjoy it more with a knowledgeable guide.'

'I'm sure I should. Let me return your hospitality by giving you lunch at the Faculty Club,' she suggested. 'I have reciprocal membership through a club I belong to in London.'

'OK, let's make that a date. How about tomorrow?'

'I know I'm tied up tomorrow and my engagement diary is in my other bag,' she said.

Both these statements were white lies. Although, so far, she liked everything about him, it was possible that if he had plans to end the evening in a way unacceptable to her, this would be their first and last date.

The advertisements in the *West Ender* might give a false impression of the moral climate in Vancouver. She didn't know how it compared with the fairly free and easy attitude among her age group in Europe. She herself would never consider making love on a first date, although she knew that one couldn't always write off a man who tried a heavy pass. A lot of them felt it was expected of them.

'We can fix it later,' he said easily.

It was a remark which suggested he expected to be seeing the inside of her suite before tonight's date was over. Not that he knew she had a suite. The hotel had a restaurant and snack bar and not all its rooms had self-catering facilities. She had asked for a kitchen because she liked cooking for herself and she needed the living area to work in.

'You didn't finish telling me how you got into designing,' he said. 'Talking about your dolls' house sidetracked us into architecture.'

Alex sipped her wine before she said, 'When I was ten my parents were killed in an accident. I went to live with an aunt and her family. They were terribly kind to me but it was a different way of life. My only link with the past was Red Gables, my dolls' house. I spent hours making things for it; tiny curtains and cushions and so on. Then one of my cousins who was interested in woodwork let me borrow his tools to make little pieces of furniture from empty cigar boxes. By the time I was sixteen I could make almost anything I needed to change the décor, and I still had a hundred ideas I wanted to try out. There was never really any doubt where my *métier* lay. How about you? What drew you to oceanography?'

'There's a certain parallel between our childhoods,' he

told her. 'I was also in a situation which wasn't comfortable for me. Like you, I needed a bolt-hole. Mine was museums. We were living in Europe and sometimes in New York at that time. I was able to wander around some of the world's finest natural history and science museums. There were other influences as well. The vacations I did spend in Vancouver convinced me that I didn't want to live in a climate as wet as western Canada. My preferred clothing is a pair of shorts, not a raincoat and an umbrella, which is *de rigueur* here for much of the year.'

She had assumed he was single but, although he had checked her status, she hadn't asked about his. She did now.

'Can you go wherever your work takes you? You have no dependents to consider?'

'No, I have neither ex-wives nor children. If I had I shouldn't have qualms about uprooting them. I don't believe it does any harm to move children around the world. It's probably good for them; stops them becoming insular, like some Vancouverites who think the world begins and ends in BC. What children need more than geographical stability is domestic stability. Parents who love them and each other. Wouldn't you agree?'

Alex nodded, remembering the security of her life before the accident, and how all her cousins, including the two adopted ones, had grown up with the daily evidence that their father and mother were a devoted couple whose love for each other was the mainspring of their existence.

However, marital happiness was not a matter she wanted to dwell on. She steered the conversation away from that topic by asking, 'Do Vancouverites tend to be insular? They don't appear to be reserved. All the ones I've met have been very friendly and outgoing. Which considering that I'm an outsider coming in and taking some bread out of their mouths, as it were, is a little surprising. I'd expected a certain hostility.'

'Most people find it quite difficult to be hostile to an

attractive young woman,' was his quizzical comment. 'If you were going to have a problem here, I'd have thought it would be fending people off. Or are most of the men you encounter in your line of business not interested in women?'

'Some of the designers and antique dealers aren't. But most architects and contractors are, or were before they became husbands and fathers. I haven't had to repulse any unwelcome advances, if that's what you mean. Not so far,' she added, with a direct glance, hoping he would get the message that she hoped she would never have to.

A slight rather enigmatic smile touched the corners of his mouth.

'Maybe not in Vancouver, but elsewhere I'm sure you've had plenty of practice in putting down guys who get out of line,' he answered. 'I can see you're not engaged——' with a glance at her ringless left hand '—and presumably there's no one special in your life at the moment.'

'If there were, I shouldn't be having dinner with you. I have rather old-fashioned ideas about that sort of thing.'

'That's what I thought you would think. I have an idea we share the same views on a number of important issues.'

'Really? How can you tell on so short an acquaintance?'

'I've been trained to take notice of details. For example, I can tell you don't live solely on coffee and junk food by the condition of your hair and skin. You're not easily led, or not by the fashion pundits. You aren't wearing your hair the new way and your clothes aren't the latest fashion. I intend that to be a compliment. I prefer classic simplicity to the whims of the fashion designers. Most men my age do. You look great.'

The air-conditioning made the bar a little cool. She had kept on her cashmere jacket but thrown it open. His dark eyes appraised the curves under the fluid black silk.

Aware that her colour had risen, she said, 'Thank you. The way I dress is dictated by my job. Most of my private clients are quite rich, and their wives can afford to buy from the top designers' current collections. I can't, so I have to settle for a few good clothes which will stay in style for several years. It's the way successful men dress and always have. Perhaps you haven't had that nice grey suit very long but I'm sure you'll still be able to wear it in five years' time, perhaps even ten years ahead.'

He glanced down at his suit. 'I'm hoping for a lot more mileage out of it than that. I don't wear a suit too often. Jeans or chinos are more my style. What do you do in your spare time apart from walking, Alexandra?'

'I read. I tap dance. In London I go to a dance studio where, depending on how busy I am, I take two or three classes a week. Here, the only classes I've found are at the YMCA on Burrard.'

By now the bar was overlooking English Bay. His glass was empty, hers almost so.

'You'll have another glass, won't you?' he asked her.

'Thank you.' She watched him catch the waiter's eye and by a slight change of expression summon the man to their side.

She had met a number of men in positions of power and influence and she recognised the relaxed yet authoritative manner of someone accustomed to quick, efficient service. Laurier had stated his lack of interest in the business built up by his grandfather, but obviously he had inherited some of the qualities of the founder of the family fortune. Putting two and two together, she was fairly certain that the part of Vancouver where his grandmother lived was the exclusive Shaughnessy neighbourhood which did have a bus route leading to downtown Granville Street.

After her tour of the important city-centre landmarks, Alex had made a point of exploring the élite residential districts to make notes on the type of houses preferred by the city's top people.

Many of the newly rich seemed to live in West

Vancouver. The old guard were concentrated in an area of quiet, tree-lined streets of which the hub was The Crescent.

In the spring of 1909, she had discovered, the Canadian Pacific Railway, which had received land grants from the new City of Vancouver in return for extending its line, had announced a sale of building lots, none smaller than half an acre, in an area called Shaughnessy Heights. Here the first of the city's millionaires had built their impressive mansions, many in the style known in England as Stockbroker's Tudor, and in Canada as Tudor Revival.

Alex strongly suspected that one of those rambling old houses was Laurier's ancestral home. If her supposition were correct, it must make him one of Vancouver's eligible bachelors, and she wondered why he was still single.

Unless, in spite of his remark about their sharing the same views, he was actually an inveterate womaniser, the more dangerous because he camouflaged his predatory nature with a *simpatico* manner.

I really know nothing about him except that he's the most attractive man I've ever met, she reminded herself.

However, as the evening progressed, she found that it wasn't only his physical presence which attracted her. The more he revealed of his mind and his sense of humour, the more she was drawn to him. It had been a long time since she had laughed as often as she did during dinner.

At first, when their taxi from the Sheraton turned downhill, she thought they were going to one of the restaurants on Denman, a neighbourhood shopping street which spanned the West End from the inner harbour, which she saw from her window, to the outer harbour, English Bay.

It was in that direction they turned, but not to stop along Denman. To her surprise the taxi went as far as Beach Avenue where it swung in the direction of the park.

'That's the old Sylvia Hotel which my grandmother remembers as a smart place to lunch in the thirties,' said

Laurier, pointing out a building, its façade thickly covered with the red leaves of what Alex knew as Virginia creeper. 'It wouldn't be old in Europe but here it's a "heritage" building. Some Europeans feel uncomfortable in a place with no pre-Victorian architecture. Do you?'

'I haven't so far, but don't you think cities are like people? It takes time to get to know them and sometimes one's first impressions change from good to bad or vice versa. Two weeks isn't really long enough to form a lasting opinion. At the moment it's all new and fascinating to me.'

They were entering the edge of the park on the side which she hadn't yet explored. She assumed they must be heading for the famous Lion's Gate suspension bridge which took traffic across the First Narrows. But the most direct route to the bridge cut through the centre of the park and now they were passing along what she knew from studying her map to be a quieter circumference road.

She had heard Laurier ask the driver to take them to the Teahouse Restaurant and was wondering if it were a Japanese place and he was a *sushi* addict when the taxi turned off the main road into a parking area between an expanse of grass and a low building somewhat resembling an old-fashioned glass conservatory.

'This is Ferguson Point,' said Laurier, when the taxi had dropped them and they were pausing to admire the view across the moonlit ocean to the shimmer of lights on the far side of English Bay.

Rather to Alex's relief, when they entered the restaurant she saw at once that it wasn't a *sushi* place. Although she liked to watch the artistry with which an expert *sushi* chef cut the fine strips of raw fish and arranged it on tiny rice patties bound with ribbons of seaweed, she thought *sushi* looked better than it tasted.

'I thought as we met in the park it would be appropriate to dine here,' he told her, after they had been shown to a table on the seaward side of the conservatory. 'When I was in my early twenties there wasn't a wide choice of restaurants, but now Vancouver has every kind of eating place from Mexican to Lebanese. In this restaurant the emphasis is on seafood and French dishes, which seemed a safer bet than Chinese food, which I like but you may not.'

'I do, as it happens, and in Vancouver I gather you get all the regional varieties—Hakka, Szechuan and so on.'

He nodded. 'Have you been to Chinatown yet?'

'Yes, and I found the shops fascinating. There were quite a few vegetables I didn't recognise—and what amazing things the meat shops do with ducks and chickens!'

With other men she had dated in her early twenties, and even with Peter, her long-term partner, there had been times when the conversation had dried up; or she had found herself secretly bored by a subject of interest to them but not to her.

With Laurier the evening seemed to pass in a flash. They had so many interests in common. He was interested in her work and she in his.

It was almost midnight when a taxi brought them back to her hotel.

'Wait for me, please,' Laurier said to the driver, before he got out of the car and offered his hand to help Alex step on to the pavement.

'I'll see you as far as the lift,' he told her.

'I have enjoyed myself, Laurier. Thank you,' she told him warmly, as they crossed the lobby.

'We must do it again—soon,' he answered.

He pressed the lift call button and offered his hand. He was still holding hers in his strong clasp when the doors slid apart.

'Thank you again. Goodnight.'

She tried to withdraw her fingers but he wouldn't release them. 'Will you be walking at your usual time or later tomorrow?'

'At the usual time—unless the weather has broken.'

'Then I'll see you on the sea wall. Goodnight, Alexandra.'

He watched her until the lift closed and bore her upwards.

As, a few moments later, Alex unlocked her door, she thought what a strange society it was in which two unattached people who would have enjoyed spending the night together parted from each other. Not that everyone in their shoes would have done so, of course. But she and Laurier had.

Perhaps it was the sudden death of both her parents when they were not so many years older than she was now which made her more conscious of her mortality than most people in their twenties. She had grown up with the awareness that a long span of life should never be taken for granted, and that, even when life was long, for an unmarried woman the power to attract lovers diminished as the years passed.

So why, while she had that power, had she passed up the chance to use it—in the subtlest possible way—and make a memory to warm her in the years ahead when no one wanted to share her bed?

Analysing her behaviour as she hung up her clothes, she supposed the basic reason had nothing to do with morals. If she were honest with herself, she didn't feel it would have been wrong to ask Laurier up for coffee and to succumb to the pass he would almost certainly have made if she had. The restraining influence had been the fear that, if she showed herself willing to make love as soon as this, he would think less of her, just as she would have been disappointed in him if he'd been in too much of a hurry to get her into bed.

Nevertheless, all evening, underlying the exchange of personal information and the discussion of subjects of mutual interest, there had been a strong undercurrent of male-female attraction.

Had they been members of a primitive society with no taboos against doing what came naturally, by now they would be in each other's arms in the shadow of a palm or the darkness of a thatched hut. Instead, because they belonged to a sophisticated society with complex rules and lingering traces of the old double standard, they were each going to bed alone, in a state of unsatisfied desire.

Trying to close her mind to a disturbing image of Laurier taking off his clothes and padding around his bedroom, his tall, lean, exercised body moving with the supple grace which had turned her on the first time she saw him, Alex found it hard to concentrate on less inflammatory thoughts.

At two o'clock in the morning, unable to sleep, she stood on the balcony of her suite, sipping a glass of milk which she hoped would prove soporific, and gazing at the spectacular view of Vancouver by night.

Even at this hour North Vancouver was a shimmering, glittering blaze of light on the far side of the black-satin sheen of the harbour. Close to the south shore the water was patterned with rippling streamers of vivid colour, the reflections of the lights on the floating petrol stations where the tug-boats and motor cruisers refuelled. Mundane by day, at night the stations were beautiful, the one furthest out, Shell, making a ribbon of gold, pink and bronze light. Chevron and Gulf combined violet and lilac and Esso trailed a fuchsia reflection with azure borders. Beyond them was the winking red light of a marker buoy.

Although only a few lights showed from the towers of apartments, whole floors were brightly illuminated in many of the office buildings. Hundreds of fluorescent tubes left burning while the offices were deserted had seemed a great waste of energy until it occurred to her that here in Canada the great rivers flowing seaward were the main source of power.

At night the temperature dropped. After a short time

outside she began to feel chilly and returned to the living-room, but it was useless to go back to bed until she had made up her mind what to do about Laurier.

Now the euphoric mood induced by the wine and his company had worn off, she knew it was crazy to go on seeing him. Even at this stage she foresaw a real danger of losing her heart to him, and for her the outcome of love wouldn't be happiness. It could only be heartache.

Was a brief autumn idyll worth the emotional upheaval?

Her heart said yes but her head took the negative view. And was it really her heart which yearned for an end to the lonely nights of the past three years? Or was it only a primeval instinct at work, trying to make her conform to the pattern followed by generations of her female ancestors?

The next morning, instead of using the underpass, she followed the path which went round the stretch of water called Lost Lagoon. She had asked Laurier why it was called that. He had said the name came from verses about the lake written by a Canadian poetess, Pauline Johnson, who was buried in Stanley Park.

As she walked, Alex wondered if he would conclude that her absence from her usual route was because she had overslept. She wondered when he would call her, and how difficult it would be to give him the brush off.

Because that was the only sensible course of action. She had behaved very foolishly by accepting his initial invitation; to continue the association would be madness. It wouldn't be fair to him either.

On the way back to her apartment, she put a quarter into one of the newspaper vending boxes which were a frequent sight on the streets of Vancouver and took out the *Globe and Mail*, Canada's national newspaper.

After reading it at breakfast for two weeks, she had noticed that most of the news was from Toronto where the paper was published. Even Ottawa, the capital, appeared to take second place and Vancouver, in spite of its million-plus population, had a much smaller share of the *Globe*'s columns.

Laurier had explained this imbalance to her by pointing out that Canada's centres of population were concentrated along its southern border, leaving most of the northlands an empty wilderness. Geographically, Vancouver was closer to the cities of America's Pacific coast than to Toronto and Montreal. It was therefore hardly surprising that in Toronto it was regarded as an unimportant place out west.

'Which, as you can imagine, breeds a good deal of resentment among Vancouverites,' he had added, when the subject had come up during dinner last night.

As she chopped a fresh grapefruit and added peanuts, blueberries and a generous dollop of yogurt, she tried not to remember how much she had enjoyed discussing Canada with someone who could answer her questions knowledge-ably but without the parochial prejudices of a man who had never been anywhere else.

She had finished breakfast and was on her way to the shower when the telephone rang. She felt sure it could only be Laurier and braced herself for the difficult necessity of assuming a coolness at variance with her manner towards him when they parted in the lobby last night.

However, when she lifted the receiver and gave the number of her suite, a voice boomed, 'John Kassinopolis. How are you, Alex? How are things going?'

'Oh ... Good morning, Mr Kassinopolis. The work is going well. I'm ahead of the schedule I set myself.'

'Splendid. No problems at all?'

None in my working life, was her thought. Aloud, she said, 'No, everything has been running very smoothly. I've finished working out the basics. Now I'm tackling the details.' She pronounced the last word in the North American way with the emphasis on the second syllable.

'You must have been working hard. You've only been there two weeks.'

'It's not hard to work hard when you like your job as much as I do. My work is a holiday to me.'

'Mine, too,' was his comment. 'But work can be an addiction. Don't become a workaholic. What are you doing this evening? Do you have a date?'

'No, I'd intended working tonight.'

'Have a working dinner with me. I'll send a car for you at seven.'

'Are you in Vancouver?' she asked, in surprise.

'No, I'm calling from Toronto but I'll be in Vancouver late this afternoon.'

CHAPTER TWO

'WOULD you like to look at the models and approve what I've done so far?' Alex asked. 'They're at my hotel. I find it easier to work here than in the office the architects put at my disposal.'

'You don't like the office? Get them to find you another.'

'No, no—it isn't that. It's a very nice office. I just prefer working at home or wherever I happen to be living. It makes it easier to have a snack lunch, or to work late.'

'That's a sure sign of workaholicism. A young woman your age shouldn't make a habit of working late.'

'I don't. I was out to dinner last night.'

'I'm glad to hear it. However much you enjoy what you do, it's important to keep a balance. I found that out when my wife died. I realised I'd missed a great many pleasures we should have shared. I'll be there to look at the models at seven. Goodbye.' John Kassinopolis rang off.

She had known that he was a widower. The first time they met, at the party, he had made some reference to his wife. When Alex had glanced round the room and asked, 'Which is your wife?' a sad look had crossed his face. He had answered,

'Mary died eight months ago.'

The way he still counted the months since her death, rather than saying 'last year' or 'last fall', had given Alex the impression that Mary Kassinopolis had meant more to him than was sometimes the case when married couples reached middle age.

She had placed him in his early fifties. His hair was grey but still thick and although he carried the evidence of too

40

much rich living round his waistline, he was a dynamic man who would be attractive to women closer to his age. It had surprised her to learn that he had no children, no sons or daughters to inherit his empire of hotels and restaurants.

Guessing he would probably stay in a suite at the imposing Hotel Vancouver or perhaps the more modern Four Seasons, she wondered if it might make a pleasant change for him to have a home-cooked supper. Eating in the restaurants of luxury hotels was a treat for those who rarely did it but, like everything else in life, it must lose its edge if one did it all the time. She wondered how long it had been since he had munched corn on the cob. It wasn't the kind of thing they served in elegant restaurants; it was too messy.

Deciding to take a chance on her judgement of his character, she looked up the number of the Four Seasons and asked if they were expecting Mr John Kassinopolis to check in later that day. Told that they were, she asked them to have a message given to him as soon as he arrived.

'Would you tell him that Miss Clifford would like him to be her guest for dinner tonight and would he please wear casual clothes if he has some with him,' she said to the girl who took her call.

During the morning she went out to post a letter to her aunt and to shop for the meal that evening. When she returned to her apartment she found that a beautiful white cyclamen had been delivered during her absence.

A card was tucked among the leaves. It read, *I guess you overslept after all. I'll call you later. L.*

Alex gazed at the delicate flowers poised on their tall stalks, like a cloud of white butterflies, above the heart-shaped leaves with their grey-green markings. Was it coincidence that he'd chosen a white cyclamen, or did he share her preference for white flowers—white lilac, snowdrops, lilies of the valley, white roses and narcissi?

When she was a little girl, she had always been made to write thank-you notes for birthday and other parties. She had seen her mother writing to thank friends for dinner parties. Having kept up the habit inculcated in childhood, she would have written a thank-you note to Laurier immediately after breakfast had she known his address.

The arrival of the pot plant made it imperative to write to or telephone him, rather than waiting for his call. If he suggested another date, she would claim to be madly busy. At a pinch she could say that her boss was in town and didn't like her designs which would have to be completely revised, necessitating a lot of overtime work.

For the second time that morning she opened the telephone directory. There were 138 Taits in the book, several of them with addresses she knew to be in the Shaughnessy area. With the first one she tried the number rang for some time. She was about to hang up when the ringing stopped and a woman's voice said, rather breathlessly, 'Hello?'

Alex said, 'Good morning. I'm not sure if I have the right number. Is that the home of Mr Laurier Tait?'

'It is. Is that Miss Clifford?'

Startled, Alex said. 'Yes—but how did you guess?'

'By your English accent. Laurier mentioned you to me at breakfast this morning, Miss Clifford. I'm his grandmother, Barbara Tait. I'm afraid he's not here right now. Shall I ask him to call you back as soon as he comes in? I'm expecting him for lunch.'

'No, thank you, that isn't necessary. I have a tight schedule of business appointments today and I'm busy this evening as well. I just wanted to find out his address so that I could write a note to thank him for dinner last night, Mrs Tait.'

'What nice old-fashioned manners, Miss Clifford. Not many of your generation go to that trouble. But my grandson tells me you are an unusual young woman. I hope we shall meet before you finish your assignment in Vancouver.'

Alex found herself saying, 'Thank you. I hope so, too.' To avoid being drawn into further conversation, she added, 'Goodbye, Mrs Tait,' and replaced her receiver.

At two minutes past seven the desk clerk announced Mr Kassinopolis's presence in the lobby.

'Would you ask him to come up, please,' said Alex.

Taking her key with her, she walked along the corridor to meet him when he stepped out of the lift. She was wearing white cotton trousers, lined with fine batiste to make them hang well, and a white cotton shirt with a gold kid belt and gold sandals on her slim bare feet.

As the door slid aside and he saw her waiting for him, a smile spread across John Kassinopolis's broad face. Although no doubt he could be severe when he chose, every time she had met him his manner had been cheerful and relaxed, apart from the brief look of sadness when he had remembered his wife.

'How are you, Alex? How are you liking Canada?' he asked, taking her hand between his.

'I'm fine, thank you, and Vancouver is great. Wait till you see my fabulous view.' As she led the way back to her room, she asked, 'How long are you here for?'

'I have afternoon appointments in San Francisco.'

She unlocked her door and stood aside. 'Please go in.'

He had, she noticed, obeyed the request in her message. In place of the suits in which she had seen him previously, tonight he was wearing a light-coloured blazer over an open-necked shirt.

It wasn't the view which caught his attention as he walked into the living area but the models for the penthouse suites. Two were on the long low table in front of the sofa and the others on a built-in desk.

As he began to study them, she said, 'What would you like to drink, Mr Kassinopolis? I have only a limited choice . . . gin, wine or beer.'

'I'll have a beer, please—and there's no need to be formal. Call me John,' he instructed, without looking up from the first model.

When she brought the beer to him, he was looking at the second model.

'You must have been working very hard in the time you've been here. I didn't expect to find this much progress.'

'I couldn't have done it without the co-operation of your architects. They've been amazingly helpful considering I'm an outsider. It would be natural for them to resent that a little. There are plenty of good designers in Vancouver who would have jumped at this commission.'

'There are, and if I hadn't happened to meet you in London probably a local designer would have been given the job. As a general rule, I'm in favour of employing the people on the spot. But as you know from your brief, these suites are intended to accommodate an élite international clientele who have travelled all over the world and have the most sophisticated taste. I wasn't satisfied that any of the designers in this city had the fine, original taste to provide an appropriate background for people at that level. After seeing your work, I felt you had. These confirm that I was right.'

'They're barely half-way to completion. The basic layouts are there, and the colour schemes, but none of the details which are so important,' she said. 'I'm lucky that an antique dealer in London who supplies a lot of my accent pieces gave me a letter of introduction to a dealer here who handles the same sort of things or knows where they might be obtained.'

While he drank the beer he asked questions and she gave him the answers, explaining aspects of the designs not yet on view in the models.

'Where did you have them made?' he asked.

'I made them myself. It's not difficult when you know how.'

'You mean you did the actual construction?' He rapped the outer walls lightly with his knuckles.

She nodded. 'Why not? Using a saw and a screwdriver isn't the prerogative of your sex. If a woman can cut out and sew a dress, she can construct a dolls' house which is, fundamentally, what these are except that they're viewed from above rather than from one side. Would you like to come to the table? I think dinner is just about ready.'

Five minutes later, wiping melted butter from his chin with one of the two large napkins she had bought specially for the occasion, he said with a grin, 'I used to love corn as a kid but I haven't had any in years.'

'It's very cheap at the moment. I have it almost every day, and I'm practically living on salmon because that's a bargain here, too—compared with the price it is in England. I've found the fruit excellent. Huge Milwaukee plums, the size of apples, and big juicy blueberries. The only thing I can't track down is civilised bread. The supermarkets are full of horrible soft factory bread instead of real bakers' loaves with a chewy crust.'

'You don't look as if you ever touch bread,' he remarked, glancing at her figure. 'I wish I could keep my weight down. Maybe I should take up jogging.'

'I shouldn't if I were you. It jars people's joints. Walking is better, especially for anyone not used to regular exercise. Perhaps you should spend less time in limousines and more on Shanks's pony,' she suggested, with a twinkle. 'Did you walk here or come by car?'

'I came by car,' he admitted. 'I guess you're right. I

should get around on foot more. I've fallen into bad habits.'

'Did you go in for sports as a young man?' she asked, immediately regretting that she hadn't phrased the question more tactfully. Although he was old enough to be her father, he might not like to be reminded that he was closer to old age than youth. For some men and women in their fifties, age was a sensitive subject.

But John showed no sign of resenting the way she had phrased the question.

'No, I was always too busy making a buck and studying at night school to have time for football or baseball or any other sports,' he answered. 'My parents were Greek immigrants. I was born on the lower East side of New York, and I was determined to make it to the upper East side, which is where the rich live.'

'I didn't realise you were an American. I thought Toronto was your home town.'

'My wife was from Toronto. Eventually she inherited her parents' house and we moved there. By that time I could live where I wanted and Toronto has a lot going for it. It's a big, modern city, but it's cleaner and has less crime than most cities that size. Mary had always had a hankering to go back and I wanted her to be happy during the times I was away. When you've had a driving ambition, it's hard to know when to slow down. I went on working harder than was necessary, making money we didn't need and which couldn't buy health for my wife when she got sick. For her last few months we were together all the time. I realised how much I'd missed because of my obsession with material success. For a while after she died I went back to working twelve and fifteen hours a day. Then I made myself slow down and take time for the things Mary taught me to enjoy with her.'

'What kind of things?' asked Alex.

'Listening to music . . . looking at paintings . . . enjoying nature. But it's not the same, doing it alone. Have you been married, Alex?'

She shook her head. 'I had a two year relationship with someone, but it came to an end. I went to Florida to design a winter house for some English people, and when I came back my friend was involved with someone else. Perhaps it was too much to expect him to be waiting for me. I can't pretend it broke my heart,' she added cheerfully. 'We had had our differences for some time. I think I'm naturally solitary.'

As she rose to clear away the first course, he asked, 'Who took you to dinner last night?'

'An oceanographer.'

'From UBC?'

'No, he works in Hawaii.'

'Did he send you the flowers?' he asked, looking at the cyclamen she had placed at the far end of the dining-table.

Yes. Isn't it a beautiful plant?'

He watched her taking a casserole out of the oven. 'I imagine it's intended to convey he thinks you're beautiful.'

'I think it's more probably intended to personalise the suite, which it does. Usually, if I'm going to be somewhere for several weeks, I buy some pot plants myself to give where I'm living a homelier atmosphere. I don't know why I haven't done that this time. Probably because plants are heavy to carry and I haven't a car. I find, living in the West End, I don't need one; Vancouver has a very good bus service. I supposed it's been years since you travelled by public transport?'

'Some time, yes. But I haven't forgotten what it's like on the New York subway in rush hour,' he said, with a grimace. 'An eternity of that experience is my idea of hell.'

'I agree. The rush hour on the tube in London is equally horrible. Did you know the late night buses here are called the Owl Service? I like that.' She flashed him a smile. 'The other day I saw motorists stopping to let a black squirrel cross Robson Street.'

'I hope you don't use the late buses. This is a big city and a seaport which means it has its share of undesirables. If you're out alone, late, you should always take a cab.'

'Oh, I would. I'm aware of the hazards. There are parts of the city which are sleazy even by day.'

'You're a good cook,' John said approvingly, having tasted some of the casseroled beef and kidney with which she had served baked potatoes and broccoli. 'Where do marriage and children fit in your life-plan, Alex?'

She considered an evasive answer, but something prompted her to say frankly, 'They don't. I'm not going to marry. I don't believe it's possible to combine a career like mine with marriage. It may be one day but it isn't at present. I think it's a mistake to expect to have everything life has to offer. One has to choose what one wants most. For me, it's very important to be free to concentrate on my work without the kind of interruptions and distractions which married women have to cope with.'

'One thing they don't have to cope with is loneliness,' was his comment. 'I didn't know what it was to be lonely until my wife died. I do now.'

'Yes, if you've lived with someone for a long time it must leave a terrible gap,' she agreed sympathetically. 'But I've never had that experience. Apart from the two years with Peter, I've been living independently for almost ten years. I'm used to it. I like my own company.'

With the beef they were drinking red wine. He added some to her glass and recharged his own before he said, 'But you go out with men from time to time.'

'On a friendly basis.'

He gave her a thoughtful look. She was almost certain he was wondering if her definition of friendly included making love. But if that was the question in his mind, he contained his curiosity, leaving her to wonder what he did about sex. He wasn't old enough to have renounced it as a man in his sixties might if a much-loved wife died. On the other hand she had never heard or read any gossip about John Kassinopolis's private life, and he didn't seem the kind of man to have relationships with women who had any kind of ulterior motive for going to bed with him.

She wondered suddenly if, by asking him to supper, she might have given him the idea that she wouldn't object to a personal as well as a professional association with him.

Nothing could have been further from her mind. To counteract any misunderstanding which might be germinating in him, she brought the conversation back to the subject of the penthouses and kept it there for the rest of the meal. For dessert she gave him fresh pineapple with yogurt to which she had added nuts and the delicious freeze-dried banana chips she had discovered in Galloways, one of her favourite shops on Robsonstrasse, called that because of its Continental air.

The compact kitchen was visible from the dining-table and John had noticed the equipment didn't include a dishwasher. In spite of her protests, he insisted on helping her wash the dishes which she had intended to leave stacked until he had gone.

Afterwards, while they were having coffee, seated at either end of the long sofa which could be converted into a king-size bed when the suite was shared by four people, their talk ranged over various subjects but he made no attempt to revert to personal matters.

Alex had expected him to leave fairly early, but at eleven o'clock he was still comfortably ensconced at his end of the sofa, talking about the world's best hotels, most of which he seemed to have stayed at in the course of extending his own chain.

He was an interesting man to whom, normally, she

would have listened intently. Tonight, because she had lost so much sleep last night, she found herself swallowing yawns and fighting against increasing drowsiness.

It was only when she heard him say, 'It's time I was on my way and you were in bed,' that, to her horror, she realised she had been asleep. Perhaps only for a few moments, but to nod off for even a second while he was talking—could anything be more embarrassing?

John didn't seem to be offended. He said, 'I'm sorry. I forgot you were out late last night and needed to catch up your sleep.' As he rose and she stood up with him, he went on, 'That was a great dinner, Alex. I appreciate your invitation and I'll hope to enjoy some more of your cooking another time. Meanwhile thank you for a very pleasant evening.'

'I enjoyed it, too,' she told him, still appalled by her lapse.

As she followed him to the door, he said, 'I hope you use the security lock at night.'

'Yes, I do—and there's also a peephole for seeing who is there if anyone knocks on the door.'

He opened the door and turned to her. 'A girl on her own can't be too careful.' He paused, looking into her eyes. He was not a tall man like Laurier. There was little difference in their heights. 'If I'd had a daughter she would have been around your age. Spending this evening with you makes me regret more than ever that a daughter is one of the good things in life which I've missed. Goodnight, Alex.'

To her surpise, he laid both hands on her shoulders and brushed his lips to her cheek.'

Then he walked away to the lift.

The next morning she received a florist's arrangement of pink carnations and roses with a card bearing the brief message, *Thank you. JK.*

She appreciated the gesture. But although his flowers

must have cost as least five times as much as the pot plant, they wouldn't last as long nor did they please her eye in the same way as the cyclamen did.

A few minutes after the arrival of the flowers, the telephone rang.

She picked up the receiver. 'Hello?'

'Alexandra, are you OK?'

At the sound of his voice her heart gave a peculiar lurch. 'I'm fine, thank you, Laurier. How are you?'

'Fine. When you didn't show up this morning I thought maybe you were sick.'

She had already rehearsed how to deal with this call, if and when he made it. She said pleasantly, but with a businesslike briskness in her tone, 'I don't always go the same way. This morning I walked on the English Bay side of the park.'

There was a pause before he said, 'Thank you for your letter. I was going to call you yesterday but I got tied up. Listen, this fine weather may not last too much longer. The forecast for tomorrow is rain. My half-brother owns one of the smaller Gulf Islands. It doesn't take long to get there by plane. Can I persuade you to take a long lunch break and come for a picnic over there?'

Alex steeled herself. 'It's very nice of you to suggest it, but I'm afraid that's impossible. I have engagements today which I can't possibly cancel.'

Deliberately, she didn't add, 'I'm sorry. It would have been fun. Perhaps you could show me the island another day,' as she would, had she wanted to see him again.

'Oh . . . that's a pity,' he said slowly. 'How about dinner tonight?'

It was terribly hard not to weaken but she forced herself to say coolly, 'I'm busy this evening as well. The man I'm working for arrived in Vancouver late yesterday and that means extra meetings and possibly some urgent alterations to my designs as they stand.'

'I see. That's too bad. I was hoping to show you some of my favourite places. How long is your client staying in BC?'

'I'm not sure. But my time here is limited and my social life has to take second place to my job. I'm a dedicated career girl, you know. My work means everything to me.'

There was a longer pause this time during which she was tempted to end a painful conversation by saying briskly, 'I can't talk now. I'm busy. Goodbye.'

But having already handed out a fairly obvious brush-off, she couldn't quite bring herself to utter the *coup de grâce*.

While she was biting her lip in nervous hesitation, he said, 'My work is important to me, but I wouldn't say it meant everything. There are other things I rate equally highly. However, I mustn't delay you when you're busy. Goodbye, Alexandra.'

Without waiting for her answer, he rang off.

Alex replaced the receiver. Instead of going back to the table where she had been working, she opened the sliding glass door giving on to the balcony and stepped out into the morning sun.

There wasn't a cloud in the sky. The outlines of the mountains were sharp in the bright, clear air. She could see joggers moving along the sea wall as they did at all hours of the day. A float plane had just taken off from the harbour and was flying over the park, heading west in the direction of the islands where, she had read, many Vancouverites had summer cabins.

She would have enjoyed the experience of flying in a float plane. She would have enjoyed the picnic, and the peace and quiet of an island far from the traffic noises of the city. Most of all she would have enjoyed Laurier's company.

Suddenly foolishly, and for the first time in years, her

vision was blurred by hot tears of disappointment.

She knew she had done the right thing, the sensible thing. But it hurt more than she had expected. It hurt like hell.

On the day of her tap-dancing class, the cable TV station to which she tuned every morning for the weather forecast had prophesied a sixty per cent 'prospect of precipitation', a meteorologist's wordy way of saying rain.

However, by the time Alex set out for the YMCA on Burrard, the day's heavy showers had stopped and she didn't need to put up her umbrella.

She had started learning tap in London for exercise and for fun, and because she had always enjoyed old Fred Astaire—Ginger Rogers movies on TV. Most of Vancouver's dance studios seemed to be in the suburbs, but one day at the Central Library she had seen, pinned to a noticeboard, the autumn programme of activities at the Y. They ranged from conversational Japanese to instruction in scuba diving and three grades of tap classes. She had enrolled for the intermediate course.

The lesson lasted an hour and she learned two new steps, the six-count riff and the grapevine. At the end of the class she tied a wraparound skirt over her black leotard and black tights, and changed her black patent tap shoes for walking shoes.

'It's raining again,' she heard another girl say.

When Alex looked towards the windows she saw, by the light of a street lamp, that a slow fine drizzle was falling.

She left the building by the side exit. As she stood on the steps, putting up her umbrella, a man in a yachtsman's bright yellow foul-weather coat got out of a car at the kerbside.

She didn't look at him closely until he said, 'Want a ride?' and she realised, with a leaping pulse, that it was Laurier Tait.

'Oh . . . hello. What are you doing here?' she exclaimed, in surprise.

'Waiting for you. I felt it couldn't interfere with that all-consuming career of yours if I met you out of class and drove you home. You won't need that.'

He took the umbrella away from her, closed it and, grasping her firmly by the arm, propelled her down the rest of the steps and across the grass verge to his car, a low-slung two-seater.

Before she had recovered from her surprise, he had bundled her into the passenger seat and tossed her brolly into the space at the back.

From the Y to where she was living was only a ten-minute walk. In a car it took no time at all. Neither of them spoke. Alex was too taken aback by his unexpected appearance and the sarcastic crack about her career to know what to say.

Stealing a glance at his profile, she saw that his expression matched his tone. With his dark brows drawn into a forbidding frown, he looked much more daunting than her affable dinner companion of a few nights ago. Yet, perversely, the fact that he was annoyed with her pleased her. She had thought she was never going to see him again.

At the hotel he drove in to the basement car park.

'As I've saved you a walk on a wet night, the least you can do is to offer me a cup of coffee,' he said, as he switched off the engine.

'Yes . . . by all means,' Alex said faintly, beginning to wonder what she had let herself in for by antagonising this suddenly formidable Canadian.

In the lift she unbuttoned her raincoat. Tap dancing for an hour was strenuous exercise. Usually as soon as she got back she had a shower and then washed her leotard and tights and hung them up to drip-dry.

She had never had to deal with a situation like this before and being hot and sticky put her at a disadvantage.

When she took her key from her bag, Laurier took it from her. He unlocked the door of her suite, then stood aside for her to enter.

'I hope you don't mind instant coffee. I'll put on the kettle,' she said, going straight to the kitchen.

By the time she returned to the living area he had removed the yellow waterproof under which he was wearing a cherry-red V-neck sweater and a Madras shirt. The vivid colour suited his swarthy complexion and Indian-dark hair.

'If you'll excuse me, I'll change out of my dance gear,' she said, moving past him.

'You can do that in a minute. Right now I want an answer,' he told her curtly.

'An answer to what?' she asked, beginning to shed her raincoat.

Even in his present mood he at once moved forward to help her take off the coat which he then tossed over a chair.

'I want to know why, having spent one apparently pleasant evening with me, you then applied the cold shoulder?' he said, frowning down at her. 'I'd have had to be pretty dense not to recognise that obvious brush-off on the telephone the other morning.'

What could she say? Not 'I felt there was a danger that, if we went on seeing each other, I might fall in love with you.'

'At least you don't deny the charge,' he said, with a hint of the humour which had characterised his attitude to life during their evening together. 'I can't stand women who will never admit culpability for anything from a smashed plate to an obvious lie.'

He left her no choice but to say, 'No, I don't deny it, but that isn't to say that I owe you an explanation. I'm sorry if I hurt your feelings, but——'

'My feelings are tougher than that. Tough enough to take the truth instead of a pack of excuses about how busy you are. Even if your client is in town, he doesn't expect you to be at his beck and call all day and all evening. If dining with me was a bore——'

'You know it wasn't,' she cut in. 'But I——'

This time he cut her short. 'Yes, I do. I believe it was the best evening either of us has had in a long time. That's why I didn't expect to get turned down when I suggested we repeat the pleasure. You weren't lying when you told me you were free, were you?'

'Certainly not. I—I think the kettle is boiling.'

But when she would have turned away to deal with it, he took her by the shoulders—much less gently than John had—and stopped her.

'The coffee can wait. I want an explanation of why you changed your mind about seeing me.'

Alex resented being cornered in this high-handed fashion. She said indignantly. 'You may want one but you aren't going to get one. Please let me go.'

The next instant, instead of being held by two strong hands clamped on her shoulders, she found herself being pulled into his arms while his tall head swooped towards hers.

Instinctively she closed her eyes a second before, with stunned disbelief, she experienced the almost forgotten sensation of a man's mouth closing on hers in a long and passionate kiss. It began fiercely, almost brutally, gradually changing until he was no longer venting anger and impatience and she was no longer resisting his superior strength. In the end they were both swept away on the same tide of physical pleasure.

At last he let her go, taking his lips from hers slowly and with reluctance, and then, when she opened her eyes, letting his arms fall.

'You had absolutely no right to do that,' she said, in a low, shaken voice.

'Maybe not—but we both enjoyed it,' he answered thickly. 'Why fight the attraction between us? You know it exists as well as I do. Why pretend it doesn't, Alexandra?'

Leaving her searching for an answer, he went round the corner into the kitchen.

Alex sank into a chair, her thoughts and emotions in total confusion. She couldn't remember ever feeling this way before. No man had ever kissed her like that, not even Peter when he had been making love to her. In fact that side of their relationship had been a big let-down, which she had supposed must be her fault.

Perhaps the years of repression had something to do with it, but with one kiss Laurier had aroused sensations which were shocking in their intensity. He was almost a stranger still, yet right at this moment she wanted nothing more than to jump in to bed with him and find out if it *had* been a failure on her part that her one close relationship had never lived up to her dreams of ecstatic fulfilment.

She was vaguely aware that Laurier was opening and closing cupboards, looking for coffee powder and cups. She could see his reflection in the wide uncurtained window shared by both kitchen and living area. But she made no move to help him. She was still too stunned to have any normal reactions.

A few minutes later he brought two cups of coffee round the corner and put them on the low table.

'Have you eaten yet?' he asked her.

She shook her head.

'Do you like pizza?'

'Yes, but——'

'We have to eat and we have to talk,' he said firmly. 'If you don't want to go out again, I can drive down to one of the take-away places on Denman. It won't take fifteen minutes.'

Instinct told her that it was safer to talk from opposite sides of a restaurant table than in the seclusion of her apartment where things could get out of hand—as they already had.

'No . . . I think it would be better to go out. But I'll have to change.'

'Not for a pizza place. You look fine as you are.'

His dark gaze scanned her slim figure, making her conscious that the stretchy fabric of the leotard was far more revealing than her everyday clothes.

'I'd rather change,' she said, with a firmness to match his. 'I shan't be long, I'll take my coffee with me.' She picked up the cup and saucer and carried it into her bedroom.

Half an hour later they were at a corner table in a small, family-run restaurant in Vancouver's little Italy on Commercial Drive.

'The pasta here doesn't come out of packets. They make it in the kitchen,' he told her, when they had ordered. He glanced round the room at the few other people present. 'It's usually busier than this.'

'I expect that's because it's a wet night,' she said, making small talk, still wondering what she could say when he repeated his demand to know why he had been brushed off.

As she spoke, her elbows were resting on the edge of the gingham-covered table, with her chin resting lightly on her interlaced fingers.

In the centre of the table was a Chianti bottle lamp with a red shade hiding the bulb and diffusing a cosy red glow which burnished the bony angles of Laurier's face and made him look more than ever like the Hollywood image of a Redskin.

He moved the lamp to one side. Then he reached across the table and took hold of one of her wrists, forcing her to loosen her fingers and let him take her hand in his.

'Now tell me why you decided to end our friendship when it had barely got started,' he said quietly.

She tried to slip her hand free but he wouldn't let her. All she succeeded in doing was to make him hold it more firmly in his long, strong fingers.

'I'm not sure that I believe in friendship between people of different sexes. It usually seems to end in ... complications. And I have no time and no wish to complicate my life,' she said, avoiding his eyes.

'Look at me, Alexandra.'

The quiet command sent a queer little shiver through her. Reluctantly, her long-lashed grey eyes met his.

'I wouldn't have thought you were a coward,' he said, in a low tone. 'Have you been hurt by a man? Is that why you're afraid to be friends with me?'

She shook her head. 'It's not that. If we could be just friends that would be fine. But most men don't have friendship in mind when they date girls,' she added drily.

'No, that's true enough,' he agreed. 'And, having kissed you, I can hardly deny that I find you a very lovely and desirable girl. But I don't see women as what the feminists call "sex objects". I may have done fifteen years ago when I was a randy youngster. But I'm a man now and have been for a long time. My relationships with women have the same basis as my friendships with men. I want to be able to discuss the things which interest me, to listen to intelligent opinions, and generally "to eat, and to drink, and to be merry" together. If, in the case of women friends, that foundation leads to something more—fine. If it doesn't, that's OK, too.'

Before she could react to this statement, the proprietor brought the wine they had chosen, uncorked it and filled their glasses.

'What gave you the idea I was the kind of guy whose

primary objective was bed?' Laurier asked, when they were alone again.

'I never thought that,' she answered. 'If it had been, you would have made a pass the other night. But in my observation of other people's lives, keeping things on a friendly basis is easier said than done. Witness what happened tonight. You kissed me against my will. You might do it again.'

'I lost my temper,' he conceded. 'Your defiant attitude riled me. I think, in fairness, you'll admit that having received a metaphorical kick in the teeth for no obvious reason, I was entitled to ask for an explanation. When you refused to give one, I wanted to shake it out of you. That being *verboten*, I kissed you—to our mutual pleasure.'

'That isn't the point. I didn't want to be kissed.'

'Let's get our facts right. You didn't want it to happen but you liked it when it did. How would you feel if I were to give you my word that I won't do it again unless you make it very clear it's no longer unwelcome? Meanwhile we'll stick strictly to being friends. What do you say?'

She twisted the stem of her glass, watching the red wine gleam with rich colour in the lamplight.

'You must have lots of friends of both sexes in Vancouver, Laurier. Why do you need to add me to your circle?'

A teenage girl brought them a basket of bread, butter and dish of olives.

He thanked her and, when she had gone, said, 'In fact I'm an odd-man-out in this city now. Most of my contemporaries here are either married or between marriages. I don't belong in either group. I get a little bored listening to people talking about their children, and I've certainly no intention of being a replacement husband to a divorcee with a ready-made family.'

The *antipasto* arrived, engaging their attention for some minutes.

'You said you might have to alter your designs for the penthouses. What doesn't your client like about them?' he asked, reminding her of the excuse she had made on the telephone.

'He has approved them so far, I'm glad to say. But getting the details perfect can be very time consuming. For instance I think the penthouses should have really first-class paintings in them. The Vancouver Art Gallery has an art rental scheme, which you probably know about, which allows members of VAG to rent pictures from a large selection by living Canadian and American artists. The fee depends on the market value of the work—they include silkscreens, watercolours, graphics, oils, every medium there is. I believe the maximum charge is fifteen dollars, which is a very cheap way to enjoy fine art for three months.'

'Yes, it's an excellent idea. Are you going to make use of it for the penthouse?'

'Not exactly. Tomorrow I'm having a meeting with the director to try to persuade him to allow us to rent some of the gallery's permanent collection.'

'I imagine the temperature and lighting at the art gallery are strictly controlled to protect the pictures from deterioration. You won't be able to provide the same conditions in the penthouses. Their occupants may want them hotter or cooler than is good for valuable paintings,' he pointed out.

His immediate grasp of what would probably be the director's first and strongest objection to her proposal made Alex nod agreement and put down her fork to explain how she meant to counter that objection.

Discussing her work with someone who could take an intelligent interest but was not involved and therefore not biased in any way was a pleasure she seldom enjoyed. She forgot how the evening had begun and was conscious only of how easy and pleasant it was to talk to him.

They were starting on their lasagne when Laurier said, 'I happened to be in Vancouver when the new art gallery opened in what used to be the courthouse. It cost twenty million dollars to convert the building and it opened with a great fanfare in the fall of 1983. I went with my grandmother to the opening night gala. It was one of those see and be seen occasions which are amusing to watch.'

She had been in the gallery several times and found it easy to visualise the splendour of the opening gala with men in black tie and women in gorgeous dresses promenading up and down the magnificent circular staircase under the domed rotunda.

'I imagine Holt Renfrew and Eaton's must have sold a lot of drop-dead dresses for an occasion like that. What did your grandmother wear? Do you remember?'

'I do, as it happens, because later she made the comment that it was the oldest dress there. She bought it on a trip to Paris with my grandfather *before* the Second World War. It was made by one of the top designers of the thirties, I forget which one. Most of her clothes are from way back, although you would never know it. To a male eye they look pretty good.'

'The clothes of that period were made from superb fabrics. I have a thirties evening dress which I bought in a moment of madness at an auction at Sotheby's in London. I feel wonderful in it. Not that I've ever worn it in public— I'm not sure it would stand being dry-cleaned if I spilled something on it. It really was a crazy extravagance; I don't know what came over me. I'd gone to the auction to bid for a Lalique necklace which would have been an investment as well as a pleasure to own. The price went too high for me and I bought the dress instead.'

'Do you collect Lalique jewellery?' he asked.

She was surprised that the name of the French designer was known to him. Although a familiar name to connoisseurs of *art nouveau* jewels and glass *objets*, René Lalique wasn't widely known among the general public.

'I was lucky enough to find a few signed pieces in antique shops when I was at art school. But there aren't many dealers now who don't recognise his style and the prices have risen sky-high,' she said regretfully. 'How do you know about him?'

'My grandmother has a Lalique clock in her bedroom and various vases and ornaments. I know she'd be delighted to show them to you. Why not come and have dinner with us one evening? The house would interest you. It was designed by Maclure, who was one of the big names in architecture here and in Victoria at the beginning of the century.'

Alex knew that the city of Victoria, over on Vancouver Island, was the provincial capital of British Columbia.

She said, 'I've been wondering whether I ought to try and visit Victoria while I'm here. I've heard it described as "for the newly wed or the nearly dead". How do you rate it?'

'I've spent very little time there recently. It's a lot smaller than Vancouver. I don't think you'd find it exciting. It may be a great place to live, but there's not much in Victoria to interest a short-term visitor. I think you'd do better to go to one of the Gulf Islands first. But don't be advised by me because, as I say, I don't know Victoria that well. Ask my grandmother what she thinks when you come to dinner tomorrow night.'

'Don't you think you should consult her before inviting me to dinner?'

'I already did,' he said blandly, with a twinkle in his eyes. 'Don't look indignant. I wasn't sure I could make you change your mind about seeing me, but I was hopeful. I'm an optimist by nature. How about you?'

It was a question to which she had no ready answer. She thought about it for some moments.

'I think I'm a mixture. I don't worry about global disasters and I'm optimistic about my career because, given a basic talent, anyone can do well if they work at it hard enough.'

'Who handles your mail and so on when you're on an assignment like this? Do you have an office in London?' Laurier asked.

They talked about her work and his work for the rest of the time they were together. Later, after he had dropped her off at the hotel, Alex wondered if she had done a foolish thing in agreeing to continue their association on the terms he'd proposed.

She had little doubt he would honour his side of the bargain as long as she gave him no encouragement. But could she be sure that she wouldn't?

As she had surmised, his grandmother's house was one of the largest in the Shaughnessy neighbourhood.

Leaving the car under the *porte-cochère,* Laurier led Alex up the wide steps to a massive front door which he unlocked the pushed open for her. It gave into an unfurnished vestibule with stained glass windows on either side and an inner door which wasn't locked. This opened into a hall with a carpeted staircase as wide as the entrance steps, a corridor leading to the rear of the house and an open space with a fireplace at present filled with dried flowers arranged in a large wicker basket.

Alex's first impression was of wood; wood-panelled walls, polished parquet surrounding the rug, solid wood doors with elaborate architraves and a flight of turned wooden banisters topped by a handrail with the sheen of a new chestnut.

Mrs Tait had not heard the car arrive because she was listening to music and working on a piece of needlepoint in a plant-filled solarium at the back of the house. As she turned off the music and rose, smiling, to greet her guest, Alex was momentarily reminded of her mother who had liked to do *petit point* while listening to Chopin and Mozart.

'I'm delighted to meet you, Miss Clifford, Laurier tells me we have Lalique glass in common and no doubt many other things,' the older woman said cordially, as they shook hands.

She was tall, rather thin, with eyebrows which had remained dark while her hair turned white. Unexpectedly, she was wearing well-cut trousers with her lilac silk shirt. Her eyes were the colour of the long rope of real amethyst beads worn doubled in the opening of her shirt. She could never had been a beauty, but her eyes were lovely, even now, and enhanced by precisely the right amount of make-up for her age. Alex liked her on sight. This was the kind of woman Elena Clifford would have been, had she lived; the kind of calm, wise, shrewd person Alex hoped to be one day.

Although it was plain Barbara Tait adored her grandson, there was nothing possessive in her manner towards him; nor, unusual in grandmothers, did she drop any reminiscences of his boyhood into the conversation. She seemed to be an outward-looking woman, more interested in the future than the past.

After dinner she took Alex on a tour of the house. Laurier came with them. As she looked at the paintings and objects of special interest, Alex was conscious that he had his eyes on her.

Among the most beautiful pieces of Lalique glass which Mrs Tait had collected on trips to Europe in the early years

of her marriage was an opalescent moulded glass dish with
six mermaids bathing in sea spray. On the landing there
was a vase with two more sea maidens on it, their tails
forming handles.

'Some of the larger pieces were presents from my
husband,' Barbara Tait explained. 'I started by buying one
small scent bottle, never dreaming it would be the first of
many.'

She switched on a light at the back of a shallow recess in
the wall of her bedroom, illuminating an array of perfume
flacons in many shapes and colours: one a stylised
artichoke, another engraved and lacquered with a design of
beetles, another moulded with flying swallows.

'I hadn't realised Lalique designed that,' said Alex,
indicating the slender sapphire-blue bottle she had seen on
beauty counters from Harrods to Bloomingdales containing Worth's *Je Reviens*.

'Lalique and François Coty, the famous French *par-
fumeur*, revolutionised the perfume industry,' said Mrs Tait.
'When Coty started to use these lovely bottles for his
essences, all the other scentmakers followed his lead.
Lalique made hundreds of thousands of beautiful bottles.
Some of the rarest are the ones with what are called tiara
stoppers.'

She opened the glass door shielding the display from dust
and took down a small flacon with a stopper in the form of a
bunch of lillies of the valley.

'Like this one that Laurier found for me in a garage sale
years ago,' she said, with a smiling glance at him.

Later, as Laurier was driving her back to the hotel, Alex
said, 'That was one of the most interesting evenings I've
had in a long time. Your grandmother is a fascinating
woman.'

'She's one of my favourite people,' he agreed.

She wondered who were the others and how many young
women had been on the list, if not permanently.

When they arrived at the hotel, he unclipped his seatbelt and reached into the back of the car.

'I thought you might like to borrow these for a while,' he said, handing her a binoculars case.

Ever since her arrival she had been wishing she possessed a pair with which to study, in close-up, parts of her spectacular view.

'How thoughtful of you. I'd love to borrow them,' she said gratefully.

As he had on their first date and last night, he saw her to the lift.

'Goodnight, Alexandra. See you in the morning.'

For the next two weeks they met every morning. Soon after she had turned around at the gun, the now familiar shadow on the asphalt would make her look over her shoulder and bid him a smiling good morning. For the rest of the way to the Rowing Club, Laurier would walk beside her.

The dry, bright, summery weather continued. Nevertheless it was autumn. Each morning, before the sun rose, the air had a sharper nip in it.

One day, after Alex had started to wear a track top over her T-shirt and had remarked that her hands had been cold on the outward walk, Laurier surprised her by producing a pair of red woollen mitts.

Touched by this second example of his thoughtfulness, she thanked him.

'Whose are they?' she asked, assuming he must have borrowed them from Mrs Tait or one of his sisters-in-law.

'They're yours. I bought them yesterday. I thought you might be too busy to remember you needed them.'

'How nice of you to remember. What do I owe you?'

'Nothing. They weren't expensive. I got them out of an On Sale bin in Eaton's basement.'

She didn't persist with her offer to pay for them. Tucking

the mitts in her pocket, she said again, 'Thank you, Laurier. My hands will be a lot more comfortable tomorrow.'

A few paces further on, he said, 'On second thoughts, you can buy me that lunch you promised me at the Faculty Club and take an afternoon off. You shouldn't go back to Europe without seeing the Museum of Anthropology. How about today?'

His reference to her return to England reminded Alex that she was more than halfway through her time in Canada. Soon she would go back to London, he would return to Hawaii. Probably they would never meet again.

She would miss his friendship very much. It might be the first and last friendship she would ever have with a man. She hadn't really believed it was possible for a single man of his age to be friends with a woman of hers, but Laurier had kept his promise. They had been to the Arts Club Theatre on Granville Island, to the Queen Elizabeth Theatre, and to the Orpheum Theatre to hear the city's symphony orchestra. Each time he had behaved perfectly. He had even agreed to let her pay for her tickets and to split the bills for the meals they had eaten.

'All right. Why not?' she agreed, seized by an uncharacteristic impulse to put pleasure before duty for once.

Laurier would have picked her up from the hotel but she knew there was a bus which would take her to the heart of the campus and she thought she might stop work early and do some shopping en route. Whenever work took her abroad, she always returned with presents for Aunt Jo and her family. Although a few hours in that crowded, noisy, untidy household were enough to make her doubly thankful for the restful, uncluttered ambience of her own home, the Fishers were the only family she had and she never forgot her debt to them.

The UBC campus on Point Grey was attractively laid

out with wide tree-lined, grass-bordered walks between the
main buildings. Swinging a tote bag containing some
presents for her cousins, Alex had no difficulty in finding
the Faculty Club for the staff of the university.

Having established her right to use its facilities, she
settled herself at a window table in the lounge, ordered a
glass of sherry and, seeing newspapers fastened to rods in a
rack near the steps to the bar, passed the time until Laurier
arrived by catching up with news from England in a day-
old copy of *The Times*.

She had been obliged to stop reading by the persistent
attempts of a young professor to get a conversation going
when Laurier came into view at the top of the stairs to the
foyer.

Had she been on her own, Alex would have waited for
him to notice her. As things were, she waved and smiled
with a good deal more animation than was strictly
necessary.

Recognising that he was outclassed by the tall striking
man on the stairs, her unwanted admirer retreated in the
direction of the bar.

'I can't blame him for trying. You look terrific,' Laurier
told her, when he joined her.

'Thank you.'

Since their meeting on the sea wall, she had washed and
blow-dried her hair, made up her face and put on a sweater
and cropped trousers which were casual but stylish.

It was the first time since his promise that Laurier's dark
gaze had lingered appreciatively on the curves of her
breasts and her small waist. Was it a sign that the amity
between them was over? That sex, lurking in the wings,
was about to make a new entrance?

She was relieved when, throughout lunch, it was men at
surrounding tables whose eyes signalled sexy thoughts.
Laurier's manner had reverted to friendliness.

After lunch they strolled the short distance to the museum. It was an unusual building inspired by the structures built by the Northwest-Coast Indians whose towering weather-bleached totem poles were displayed in the glass-walled Massive Carving Gallery.

The grotesque images carved on them, with glaring eyes and savage grimaces, made Alex vaguely uneasy. Laurier took her to admire an enormous sculpture by the Haida artist Bill Reid showing the Indian myth of the Raven discovering Mankind in a clamshell. She could see why it impressed Laurier, but it didn't appeal to her as much as two Chinese mandarins' hat buttons which she noticed in a showcase in a gallery displaying objects from all parts of the world.

Nevertheless, although he was attracted by primitive art and she wasn't, they enjoyed the two hours they spent browsing and learnt a lot from each other.

Afterwards they returned to the club for tea and continued chatting until a waitress brought round a tray of hot appetisers and they realised the teaching staff had begun to drift in for the happy hour.

Alex had ordered drinks when Laurier said, 'Next Sunday is Thanksgiving. My grandmother will be spending the day at Max's place in West Vancouver. I'm not usually here for Thanksgiving so my presence won't be missed, and I can't pretend large family parties, with my sisters-in-law barely managing to repress their mutal antipathy, are my idea of pleasure. I'm planning to spend the weekend on one of the smaller Gulf islands. I wondered if you'd care to join me?'

The question, casually put, caught Alex quite unprepared to deal with a drastic change in the tempo of their relationship.

Apart from that look before lunch, for what seemed a long time now his attitude towards her had been devoid of sexuality. Since his promise, his behaviour had been comparable with that of a happily married man thrown into close contact with a woman he liked as a person but, because of his love for his wife, not as a woman.

Now, all at once, he was looking at her in the way a man looks at a woman he finds exceedingly attractive, and she found herself reacting to that look like a girl ten years her junior. Her heart gave a peculiar lurch. Her pulses started to race. Her throat seemed to close up, making speech impossible.

Not that she knew what to say.

It wasn't the first time a man had propositioned her. In the days before her involvement with Peter, a number of men had tried to have an affair with her. None of them had been sufficiently attractive to tempt her to set aside her doubts about casual affairs. She had always felt sex without love would be a big let-down. But the practice she had had in saying no to men in her early twenties was no help in dealing with Laurier's proposition.

He lifted an eyebrow. 'You don't like small islands? Or you don't like the idea, period?'

CHAPTER THREE

SUDDENLY Alex's confusion subsided. What to say was simple because, in a flash, she knew she had never wanted anything more than to be marooned for a weekend with Laurier Tait.

'I like the idea very much. But won't your grandmother be hurt if you don't spend Thanksgiving with her? She's not young . . . and you're obviously her favourite person.'

He shook his head. 'Only one of them. She won't miss me with the rest of her brood around her. In fact she's already concluded that you and I would be spending Thanksgiving together.'

'The day perhaps . . . not the whole weekend. How will you explain that to her?'

'She won't expect an explanation. I expect she'll assume that for you it will be a day trip.'

But if she suspects otherwise she'll be bound to think less of me, thought Alex. When Mrs Tait was young, nice girls didn't spend weekends with men. They sometimes let their fiancés make love to them, but even that made them feel guilty or worried about getting pregnant.

As if he read her thoughts, Laurier said, 'You have two days to think it over. I don't want to persuade you into anything you're not certain you want to do. That's why I'm asking you now . . . not putting unfair pressure on you by touching you or kissing you.'

'You promised you wouldn't unless I showed that I wanted it,' she reminded him. 'I wasn't aware I had.'

'Not in an overt way, no,' he agreed. 'But was there ever any question about the attraction between us? I didn't think so. I thought it was just the timing which was wrong.

The first time I kissed you we hadn't known each other long enough for you to feel comfortable about it. Now we know a lot more about each other.'

The waitress returned with their drinks. Alex signed for them.

As she and Laurier leaned forward to pick up their glasses, he said quietly, 'About the only major thing left to find out is how we'll get on in bed. I don't have any serious doubts about that. Do you?'

The question was accompanied by a look which made her insides do a double flip. He might not be touching her, or kissing her, but merely by talking about their being in bed together he was putting on pressure—heavy pressure.

She gave a small shake of the head and leaned back in her chair, surprised that her hand wasn't trembling as she lifted the glass to her lips. She was trembling inside.

'Anyway, think it over,' he said. 'If, when I call you on Friday evening, you've changed your mind, that's your privilege. I'll be disappointed, but I shan't sulk, I promise you.'

On the way back to Robson Street, Alex felt sure he would kiss her goodbye. The memory of his first kiss was still vivid. She waited eagerly to feel the touch of his lips on hers for the second time.

To her surprise and disappointment he shook hands but he didn't even kiss her on the cheek.

'I'll call you late Friday,' he said. 'Thank you for lunch.'

Next morning the early mail included a letter from her aunt and the second delivery, before lunch, brought a note from Laurier, repeating his thanks for yesterday's lunch.

It was a brief courteous note of the kind he might have written to anyone who had entertained him, but she read and re-read it as many times as if it were a love letter.

She even spent time tracing the *D*, *a* and *r* from *Dear* and finding an *l*, *i*, *n* and *g* in the rest of the letter to see how

Darling would look in his handwriting. As she studied the result, and wished it were what he had written instead of *Dear Alexandra*, she could no longer deny that she was in love with him.

Friday was an interminable day. She had known she wasn't going to see him on the sea wall on Thursday or Friday because he was going on a salmon-fishing trip with one of his half-brothers. She hadn't known that two whole days without him would seem for ever.

When, soon after four on Friday, the telphone rang, she could barely restrain herself from snatching the receiver immediately. But she made herself wait until it had rung three times before she answered it.

It wasn't Laurier on the other end of the line. It was John Kassinopolis. He was calling from Toronto to ask if she would like to join a Thanksgiving weekend house party he was having there.

'It's very kind of you, John. I should have enjoyed it, but I'm afraid I've already accepted an invitation for the weekend.'

'Oh, too bad. I should have got mine in sooner. Anyway it's good you're not going to be lonesome. Not that Thanksgiving here is the big thing it is in the States, but it's no time to be on your own. I found that out last year when I was.'

He stayed on the line for some minutes, enquiring about her progress on the designs for the penthouses.

Finally he said, 'I'll be in Vancouver again soon. Maybe next week. Meantime enjoy your weekend.'

'Thank you. You, too. Goodbye, John.'

Her concentration broken by the call, Alex decided to pack up work for the day. She had designed custom-made rugs for all the penthouses and was working them in *petit point* like the Persian-style rug Elena Clifford had almost completed for the living-room of Red Gables, her daughter's dolls' house, when she was killed.

Alex never threaded her own needle with Paternayan yarn without remembering, with love, her mother's beautiful hands adorned with the antique rings bought for her by Alex's father. Whether doing embroidery, playing the piano, stroking the cat or brushing Alex's long hair, her mother's hands had always been graceful and gentle.

What would she—a dedicated wife and mother—have thought of her daughter's decision never to marry? She would have been proud of Alex's professional achievements, but would she have disapproved of her private life?

Aunt Jo had disapproved of her niece's first affair. She had never said so while Alex and Peter were living together but, after they had split up, she had accused Alex of giving way to peer pressure.

'You were twenty-two and you hadn't been to bed with anyone. So what? You hadn't had any number of life's great experiences,' she had said, in her forthright way. 'Do you know what was one of the greatest sensual experiences of my life? Sitting in the sun on a country road in France one summer, eating hunks of hot crusty bread torn from a *baguette*, with ewes' milk cheese direct from the caves at Roquefort and drinking a red Cahors wine. Then I lay on the grass and listened to the bees for half an hour. I shall never forget that picnic as long as I live—which is more than can be said for the average you-know-what.'

'Uncle Ben would be flattered,' said Alex.

Her aunt grinned, then said, very seriously, 'There've been times with Ben I shan't forget either, my dear. The point I'm trying to make is that your generation has been conned into thinking that a girl who gets to twenty-two without a lover is some kind of freak. You didn't feel you'd missed out on something vital because you hadn't been to Venice, or learnt to ski, or done any of the other million-and-one wonderful things which life has to offer. Venice could wait. Sex couldn't. It should have been the other way round. It was curiosity, and fear of being odd-girl-out, which got you into Peter's bed. You didn't love him. Don't make that mistake a second time, Alex. Sex with love is so much better than without it. Honestly.'

Remembering that advice as she worked on the miniaturised replica of the rug for a roof-top apartment in John's new luxury hotel, Alex thought, tomorrow I shall find out if Aunt Jo was right. Of course, she meant love on both sides. But even on one it must make a difference.

It was almost six before the telephone rang again. This time it was Laurier.

'Oh, hello. How was the fishing?' Alex enquired, sounding calmer than she felt.

'Good. How are you?'

'I'm fine.' *Looking forward to our trip to the island.* Should she or shouldn't she add that?

Before she could make up her mind, he said, 'I didn't get too much sleep last night. My brother has problems he wanted to talk out. So I'm going to have an early dinner and then hit the sack. Will nine o'clock be too early to pick you up—that's if our trip is still on?' He sounded confident that it was.

'Nine o'clock would be fine. According to the weather forecast it's going to be a warm, dry weekend.'

'Let's hope they've got it right. But I think we'll find ways to amuse ourselves even if it rains. Goodnight, Alexandra.'

'Goodnight.'

The caressing tone of his parting remark stayed with her all that evening.

She wouldn't have been surprised had she spent the night tossing and turning, beset by doubts and misgivings about the rightness of her decision. In fact she slept soundly and woke in a confident mood, sure that was she was about to do *was* right. Only the most reactionary and narrow-minded prude could object to her spending the next two days and nights with Laurier. That there was no commitment between them didn't alter the fact that, on her side, there was far more than physical attraction.

She loved him.

After Laurier there would be no one else. If the quality of a person's life was more important than its duration, the quality of a loving relationship must be of greater significance than how long it lasted.

As she dressed and packed her cabin bag with the few things she would need, she felt rather as she imagined World War II brides must have felt, those of them whose honeymoons had also been their husbands' embarkation leaves. Many of those young men had never returned; both they and their brides had known that was a possibility, but it hadn't deterred them from risking the pain of separation and, for the girls, the heartbreak of being widowed.

Some of them, later, had re-married. But some had lived the rest of their lives with the memory of their brief, passionate idyll. If they could survive, so could she. At least she wouldn't have to bear the anguish of living in an empty world. Laurier would still be alive. That would be some comfort.

Putting aside thoughts of the future, determined for the next forty-eight hours to live totally in the present, she put the white cyclamen in a bowl of water so that it wouldn't be drooping when she came back.

She had only been in the lobby a few minutes when Laurier arrived.

'Good morning.' He didn't kiss her, but his smile held the promise of an embrace as soon as they were somewhere more private.

'Good morning.' She didn't hide the responsive glow in her eyes.

'Is this all you're bringing?' he asked, taking the cabin bag from her.

'I didn't think I should need much.'

'You won't, but that wouldn't stop most women from packing a dozen unnecessary outfits for unlikely eventualities,' he said teasingly, as he opened the lobby door for her.

She laughed. 'That's a received idea which may be true of some older women but not of many of my contemporaries. We're into the capsule concept. Round the world with one hanging bag and one hold-all—the way men travel.'

'It must be a king-size hold-all for you to dress the way you do,' he said, watching her swing slim trousered legs into his car. 'You always look great.'

'Thank you, but so do you, and I bet you don't own a vast wardrobe.'

Laurier walked round the car and stowed her bag behind his seat. 'No, I don't,' he agreed, sliding in beside her. 'But men's clothes don't go out of fashion as quickly as women's do.'

'Intelligent women are learning that those fashions which change every season are good for the clothes manufacturers but not for them,' Alex explained. 'Very young girls get carried away by the latest fad fashions, but people of my age invest their money in classics, with just the odd bit of nonsense now and again.'

'I guess with your figure you'd look stunning in anything.' About to switch on the motor, he paused, his dark eyes taking in the silky sheen of her newly washed hair and the healthy radiance of her skin. 'You're beautiful, Alexandra ... and you always smell better than a rose garden.'

He leaned towards her and put his lips to her cheek.

'You do wonders for my morale,' she murmured, a moment before his mouth moved round to close over hers in a gentle yet sensuous kiss.

He leaned back in his seat and gave her a slow, sexy grin. 'You do wonders for me. When I'm with you, I'm like a kid of nineteen—almost permanently aroused. You don't know how difficult it's been to keep that promise I made you.'

'You appeared to find it so easy that I was beginning to wonder if you'd ever kiss me again,' she admitted.

'Were you as impatient as I was? You did a good job of concealing the fact. Let's not waste any more time. The sooner we get there, the sooner I can make love to you.'

Aware that the heat of his gaze was making her blush like a schoolgirl, she looked down at her lap. 'Isn't it a little early in the day for making love?'

Laurier's answer was, 'Tomorrow, by this time, I expect to have made love to you at least twice. Have you never made love before breakfast? It's the best way to start the day.'

His tacit reference to the fact that they both had had other relationships made her wonder what he thought about hers. Was he curious or uninterested? For her part, she couldn't help wondering about the women in his life and why none of them had lasted.

His half-brother's Cessna had a mooring south of the city not far from Vancouver's international airport where Alex had landed, never dreaming that next time she took to the air it would be with the love of her life at the controls.

'I've been flying since I was sixteen. You needn't be nervous,' he said, helping her to strap herself into the seat behind his.

'I'm not. I've always loved flying, and I'm sure you fly as well as you drive,' she answered sincerely.

During their two years together, Peter had realised his dream of owning a Ferrari. His showy, aggressive style of driving had given her many bad moments. She, more than most people, had reason to be a careful driver. Although Peter had known her history, he had never moderated his fast, risk-taking style of driving. Also he had been the kind of man who regarded all women drivers as inferior to male drivers. On the rare occasions when Alex had driven him somewhere, she had always been aware of his impatience with what he considered her over-caution.

Now that she was deeply in love for the first time in her

life, she realised just how tepid her feelings for Peter had been. He had been amusing and personable, but she had never liked him in the way she liked Laurier. Although she and Peter had been lovers, they had never really been close friends.

It was strange she should find herself thinking about the flaws in her first relationship while setting out for her second unofficial honeymoon. How wonderful it would be if this time it were 'for real' and she and the man beside her were at the beginning of a whole lifetime together.

But even if Laurier loved her, there was no possible way their lives could be made to mesh. Even with couples in the same profession, such as medicine, invariably there were problems. Oceanography and interior designing were as incompatible as oil and water.

Flying at five thousand feet above the calm Strait of Georgia between the coast of the mainland and Vancouver Island gave her a marvellous view of the Rockies and the cluster of small islands lying in the lee of the large one.

The island which was their destination was less densely wooded than its neighbours. The aircraft touched down on the water some distance away from the landing stage. As they taxied towards it, Alex saw that the cottage was considerably larger than it had seemed from the air.

When the engine was silent and Laurier had taken off his head-set, she remarked on these features.

He said, 'Most of the trees were felled when the cottage was built. Some were replaced by deciduous trees, including maples. But sunny open spaces rather than shade were the main requirement. As you'll know if you've walked the trails in Stanley Park, pine woods are dark, cool places.'

'I haven't explored those trails. It might sound silly but I'm not very keen on walking in lonely places on my own. I'm afraid that's a form of equality women are never going to enjoy to the full. Perhaps nothing bad would happen if I walked in there by myself, but I felt I'd rather not chance it.'

'I guess you're right. It could be a scary situation, running into a crackpot in there. I'll take you through some time.'

Having helped her climb down to the jetty, he unloaded her cabin bag and his grip, followed by several large cardboard boxes filled with grocery bags.

'I can manage our bags,' said Alex, picking them up.

'Thanks. I'll bring this box first and come back for the other one.' He led the way up the path from the jetty to the cottage.

It was in fact a spacious single-storey house surrounded by a wide veranda sheltered by the equally wide overhang of the low-pitched grey shingle roof.

'The place is in regular use so we shan't find it damp or musty,' he told her. 'Someone was out here last weekend. Sometimes it's lent to friends so it's rarely empty in summer. Even in winter it can be nice over here with a big driftwood fire in the hearth.'

'What about water and light? Do you have to use oil lamps and candles?'

He laughed. 'My sisters-in-law wouldn't care to be as primitive as that. They have all the usual conveniences, powered by a generator, and there's normally plenty of water, provided nobody wastes it. After an exceptionally dry spell it can be a problem, but that doesn't happen too often.'

The box he had brought up first was heavy with bottles of wine, spirits and soft drinks. Outside the door of the cottage, instead of putting it down, he said, 'The key is in my left trouser pocket. Would you mind unlocking the door?'

She put down the bags and slipped her hand in his pocket, conscious of the warmth of his body and the hardness of his hip against the back of her hand as she felt for and withdrew the key.

There was something peculiarly intimate about putting her hand in his pocket. It made her sharply aware how little physical contact there had been between them so far.

Almost as restrained as the suitor of a Victorian virgin, Laurier had scarcely touched her between their first and second kisses. Now here they were like old-fashioned honeymooners, their bodies still mysteries, their capacity to please each other still unknown.

For as she had already learned, enjoyable kisses were no guarantee that greater ecstasies must be in store. There had been none with Peter. Some pleasure, yes, but a pleasure which had always stopped short of the final transcendent bliss although, foolishly, she had been trapped into pretending that she shared his satisfaction.

She was not going to do that his time. If Laurier's lovemaking failed to stir her to the depths of her being, she was not going to pretend it had. But she hoped desperately that it would. For this time with him was her last chance to reach that high peak of delight which she knew existed. Whatever happened, it wouldn't alter her love for him and, loving him, she could never make love with anyone but him.

She unlocked the door, pushed it open and then stepped back for him to enter the house first. When she picked up the two bags and followed, the light flooding through the open door revealed a large informal living-room dominated by a wide hearth and massive chimney-breast built of roughly hewn slabs of rock.

Large, comfortable chairs and sofas invited relaxation, and the whole of one wall was covered with shelves for books and stacked magazines. The kitchen was separated from the living-room only by a long breakfast bar. Laurier dumped the heavy box on the counter and began going round opening windows and pushing back the shutters outside them. Each window framed a different view of the surrounding water and the near and far islands.

'I'll open up the bedroom and you can start unpacking while I go and fetch the food box,' he said, turning to open one of the inner doors.

Soon, from where she stood, looking about her, Alex was able to see that the room he had entered had a king-size double bed and, beyond it, sliding glass doors in a large picture window. When he had finished folding aside the hinged full-length shutters which protected the glass when the cottage was empty, she could see that, unlike any picture windows in suburbia, this one looked out on a vista supremely worthy of being painted or photographed.

In the foreground an expanse of smooth turf swept down to the water's edge; in the middle distance a sailing boat was skimming across the glittering water; in the background the steep forested heights of a much larger island soared against the blue sky.

Advancing to the threshold of the bedroom, she said, 'What a fabulous view.'

'Isn't it? And this end of the cottage doesn't have any overhang, so the morning sun streams right in and on clear nights you can lie in bed and look at the stars.'

How did he know that? Had he been told it by his relations who slept here? Or had he slept in this room before, with another girl?'

A stab of pain pierced her. She could accept that there had been others before her, but somehow she couldn't bear the idea that this island idyll wasn't an exclusive experience which no one else had shared with him.

'There's plenty of closet space.' He moved to some built-in wardrobes and opened the doors. 'The others leave some of their clothes here but there are more than enough hangers for our things. You'll find several of the drawers over there are empty. I'll be right back.'

When he had gone to fetch the second box, Alex opened her baggage and began to put away the few clothes she had brought with her. The only things which needed hanging were a spare pair of trousers and a dress of very fine silk-jersey which could be rolled in a ball and survive uncrushed. She had stuffed it into her case on a last-minute impulse. A second shirt, a thicker sweater and some underwear went in a drawer.

She had found the adjoining bathrom and was arranging her toilet things in the mirror-fronted cupboard behind the hand basin when she heard him re-enter the house, his footsteps audible as he crossed the polished board spaces between the rugs.

A sudden tremor shook her fingers, making them almost drop a tube of the French cleansing mousse she used on her face in place of soap.

'Would you like some coffee?' he called.

She raised her voice to reply. 'Yes, please.'

It was foolish to be so nervous but she couldn't help it. All her normal self-possession seemed suddenly to have deserted her. She felt as shy and uncertain as a young inexperienced girl. Would he be disappointed with her body . . . her sexual skills? Would she be able to stifle the loving words she longed to express? And to hear.

Laurier was stocking the refrigerator when she joined him in the kitchen. In spite of what he had said when they were setting out, he looked, at this moment, as if nothing were further from his mind than rushing her into bed. Her nervousness lessened a little as she watched him concentrate on arranging the supplies on the shelves of the large green fridge. There was a matching electric stove with a coffee pot heating on one of the hobs.

'You'll find mugs in the left-hand top cupboard,' he told her, over his shoulder.

She took down a couple of mugs and began to open the tall carton of milk he had left on the worktop.

'Let me do that for you,' he said. 'Those things can be tough to open. You might break a nail.'

She let him take over, thinking that he must have had some long, close relationships with the feminine sex to know that milk cartons were hazardous to fingernails. Or perhaps it was merely that his profession had made him unusually observant of the minutiae of life.

Having undone the carton for her, he returned his attention to the fridge, going down on his haunches to put heads of celery in the container at the bottom. The action drew the cloth tight across his long muscular thighs. The taut shape of his backside, the masculine outlines of his kneecaps sent an odd little shiver through her. She wanted to reach out her hand and touch the broad, powerful shoulders under the blue cotton shirt.

'You seem to have laid in enough supplies for a siege,' she remarked.

He rose from his crouching position with the lithe, elastic motion of an athlete.

'Everyone always eats twice as much over here. Let's take our coffee outdoors, shall we? I'll show you round.'

A path meandered around the edge of the island leading past weathered benches placed at vantage points. There were no flower beds or other town-garden features; only shrubs and vines planted to enhance the island's natural beauty. Here and there were rocky coves with miniature beaches.

She had seen from the air that the island boasted a tennis court.

'Do you play tennis, Alexandra?'

'I know how to. I'm not very good. I haven't played much since I left school and that's a long time ago.'

'What kind of school were you at? Co-ed? All girls?'

'All girls. But my aunt and her husband have four sons, so after I went to live with them I soon became used to a lot of boys around the place. Oh ... you have a tree-house. That was something they always wanted, but we didn't have the right kind of tree in the garden.'

'This tree-house was built for me by an old man who used to do odd jobs for my grandparents. I helped him construct it,' said Laurier, as they approached a large broad-leafed tree with a clapboard house built among its branches about twenty feet above ground. 'At first it didn't have the stairway. That was added on later. I used to get up there this way.'

Handing his empty mug to her, he strode forward and grasped a thick rope suspended from a branch above the tree-house and passing close to the open platform section. As she watched, his shoulder muscles bunched and he pulled himself swiftly upwards, hand over hand, not using his legs to aid his ascent. A few moments later he was on the platform, looking down at her.

'I'm out of practice at playing Tarzan,' he said, with a wry grin. 'I used to come up the rope like a streak of lightning.'

'You're no slouch now,' she said admiringly. Leaving the mugs on the ground at the foot of the tree, she began to climb the ladder-like stairs of which there were two angled flights.

As she joined him on the platform, he said, on a note of self-mockery, 'I was showing off. You know that, don't you? I haven't shown off to a girl for about twenty years. I guess it's because when your hair is loose and you're not wearing any make-up, you look so much younger than you are.'

In fact she was wearing make-up but applied with a very light touch.

He moved towards her, his lean hands reaching for hers. Looking down into her eyes, he said quietly, 'For someone of twenty-seven, you look amazingly . . . untouched by life, Alexandra. This can't be the first time you've been on a trip like this, can it?'

She found herself wishing it were; that the abortive affair with Peter had never happened. It had not, in retrospect, been an enriching experience.

She gave a slight shake of the head. 'No, there was someone else . . . one person . . . three years ago. But nobody since then.'

He lifted her hands to his lips, brushing kisses on her knuckles. 'You honour me,' he said gravely.

Her heart was beginning to beat in slow, heavy thumps. She found it difficult to breathe.

He placed her hands on his shoulders and put his own on her waist. For a moment longer they gazed into each other's eyes. Then he drew her close and bent to kiss her.

Minutes later, by which time her arms were locked round his neck, he said huskily, close to her ear, 'Let's go back to the cottage.'

When they reached the ground, Laurier seized her hand and, instead of following the path, took a direct line to the cottage. To keep up with his long swift stride she had to break into a trot.

A couple of yards from the steps leading up to the deck which encircled the cottage, he checked his hurried pace and, before she realised his intention, scooped her up in his arms and carried her up the steps and through the living-room to the bedroom.

There, he set her on her feet. Keeping hold of her hand, he closed and locked the bedroom door and crossed the room to pull a cord controlling a sideways sweep of billowing white voile. As the transparent folds settled into place, they gave a soft focus view of the world outside but prevented anyone seeing in.

Their privacy ensured, he led her to the bed where he sat down and drew her on to his lap. His arms round her, he buried his face against the curve of her neck and shoulder.

She felt his mouth hot on her skin and heard him say thickly, 'You're so beautiful . . .'

She woke up with no sense of time or place, only a drowsy consciousness of peace and well-being.

Lazily stretching herself, she became aware that she was lying under a warm, light covering but without her nightdress. She was naked.

In a flash, recollection returned. She knew where she was and that she had fallen asleep in Laurier's arms after the longest and most wonderful lovemaking she had ever experienced. It had been a revelation. But so emotionally and physically exhausting that afterwards, their bodies still fused, she had been unable to stay awake. Her last memory, before oblivion, was of lying with her lips an inch from his shoulder, her cheeks still damp from the tears of happiness and gratitude which had squeezed between her closed eyelids because, with him, it had been as wonderful as she had hoped.

How long had she been asleep? Where was Laurier?

Still filled with a delicious lassitude which made even looking at her watch too much of an effort, she gave a sigh of contentment and lay thinking about the care with which he had taken her, leashing his own desire until he was sure he wouldn't hurt her.

The door opened. She turned her head and watched him come to the bed and sit down beside her.

He caressed her cheek with the back of his knuckles. 'Hi!' he said softly, smiling at her.

For an answer she brought a hand up from under the cover, captured his hand and kissed it.

They spent a few moments exchanging wordless messages. Finally, he said aloud, 'Do you feel like some lunch?'

'Is it time? Why didn't you wake me when you got up?'

'I thought a nap would do you good. There's no time-schedule here. We can eat when we're hungry, sleep when we're tired and make love when we feel like it. Wash your face, put on a robe and lunch will be ready when you come through.' First bending to drop a kiss on the tip of her nose, he rose and went back to the living-room.

In the bathroom, Alex gazed in the mirror. She remembered looking at herself with the same kind of curiosity the morning after she had lost her virginity. Probably since the days when women had only polished metal in which to see their reflections, they had been staring at themselves, expecting to see some visible alteration after the momentous first time. On that occasion there had been nothing to show what had happened to her. This time it seemed to her that she did look different. Although her lashes were spiky, stuck together by the tears she had shed, she looked radiantly happy and somehow much more voluptuous than she ever had before.

As Laurier had suggested she should have lunch in her robe, she decided to do just that. Although for a long time no one but herself had seen it, she always bought pretty underwear and nightclothes for the pleasure it gave her to wear them. However, although it hadn't been necessary for her to buy new lingerie for this weekend on the island, it had seemed a good excuse to indulge in some of the glamorous things sold by a shop on Robson Street which specialised in underwear and beachwear.

One of her extravagances had been a silk dressing-gown, cut like a man's but in a small peach on cream print, the plain peach revers and cuffs piped with cream satin. It was knee length and to wear with it there was a pair of cream silk pyjama pants which, teamed with a black top, could double as evening trousers.

Laurier had laid a table out on the veranda in the sunshine. He was removing the foil from a bottle of champagne when she joined him.

'Hey, I like that,' he said appreciatively, taking in the dressing-gown. 'It has a thirties look. It must have been a grim decade but it had a lot of style.'

Alex looked with equal approval at the lunch he had set

out. It was basically a picnic, but a picnic in the grand manner.

'I don't usually eat much lunch, but today I'm starving. It must be the sea air.'

He gave her a lecherous grin. 'Or the unaccustomed exercise.'

She grinned back at him. Then her expression became softly serious. 'You were wonderful to me. Thank you.'

His eyebrows contracted in a slight frown of puzzlement. 'Weren't you expecting it to be good?'

'Yes . . . but not as marvellous as it was . . . not the first time. It was never like that for me before. I . . . I feel a new person.'

He eased the cork from the bottle, allowing only a wisp of vapour to escape before tipping a golden cascade into the long-stemmed flutes which seemed unusual glasses to find at a summer cottage. Perhaps he had brought them with him.

After standing the bottle in a bucket of ice which stood on the veranda in the shade of the table, he picked up both glasses and handed one to her.

'When you cried, I was afraid I'd hurt you,' he said, looking down at her with so much kindness in his eyes that it brought a lump to her throat.

'I was crying for happiness. I——'

She stopped short. In her confusion, she took a quick gulp of champagne. The words on the tip of her tongue had been *I love you, Laurier.* My God! What if they had slipped out? The embarrassment would have been hideous. Love wasn't part of this package, only friendship and the golden bonus of finding him a brilliant lover.

'Let's make that our toast. Happiness.' With a small clink, he touched the side of his glass to the side of hers.

'Happiness!' she echoed.

As the toast for their first shared bottle of champagne, it was well chosen. Happiness had no fixed term. It could be a single moment, an hour, a day, a long weekend, or a lifetime. For her it was this weekend . . . this one paradisean weekend. Afterwards, who could say? It was better not to think about afterwards but to live only for the present.

He had placed the chairs at right angles to each other rather than on opposite sides of the table. He drew one of them out for her.

'That looks an interesting salad,' she said, eyeing the large wooden bowl in which, as well as the usual salad ingredients, she could see avocado, peach, grapes and nuts.

'One of my sisters-in-law is a health-food crank. She doesn't approve of barbecues. Louise feeds her family on superior rabbit food, and I have to admit it's very good.'

'I thought barbecues were an integral part of North American life?'

He nodded. 'They are. Partly because it's the only way women can get the men to take over some of the cooking. However, according to Louise, not only are too many steaks and sausages bad, but if they get charred, as they frequently do, they're actually carcinogenic. The only steaks seen on her table are salmon steaks. Her family don't eat beef at all, except for calves' liver.'

'Would you accept that regime?'

'Why not? If I had an intelligent wife who had studied nutrition and wanted to keep me alive and fit as long as possible, I'd eat whatever she suggested. The soundness of Louise's theories is proved by the fact that she and her family are a whole lot fitter and healthier than Marguerite and Ian, who eat in restaurants more often then they do at home. Their children are older and have left home. Louise and Max have a larger family with two children still under ten. You must meet them. They're a fun crowd. I don't think you'd have much in common with Marguerite.'

Having helped herself to two of the pâtés he had bought, probably from La Madrague in the Granville Island market on his way downtown, Alex took a big helping of the salad.

'Why do you say that?'

'I guess because I don't like her, and you and I seem to share a lot of the same attitudes,' he answered, offering the basket of French bread to her.

'What is it about her you particularly dislike?'

'She's the kind of woman who would like anyone in a high positon regardless of their personal qualities. She spends a lot of her time in beauty salons. I suspect she's already had a couple of face-lifts. I've never known her really laugh. God knows what kind of sex life they have if Ian's not allowed to muss her hair.' He put out his hand to touch Alex's hair. 'I don't go for fancy hairdos. I like soft hair which spreads over the pillow the way yours does.'

As he withdrew his hand, she put hers up to touch the crisp dark hair brushed back from his sunburned temple.

'I like thick, springy, almost-black hair,' she murmured.

The upward movement of her arm must have outlined the shape of her breasts against the thin silk. The revers were held in place only by the sash round her waist. He reached over and slid his hand inside the top of the dressing-gown.

'You're not wearing anything under that.'

The touch of his palm against her flesh was instant excitement.

'Should I be?'

He didn't answer, his gaze shifting to her mouth, his touch becoming deliberately sensuous.

She closed her eyes for a second, amazed at the strength of the desire sweeping through her.

Looking at him, she said unsteadily, 'If you go on doing that I shall lose my appetite for food and this lovely lunch will be wasted.'

For a few moments longer his fingers lingered on her quivering skin. Then with obvious reluctance he withdrew his hand and smoothed the revers into place.

'You're right. The food won't be improved by sitting in the sun for half an hour. We'd better eat first and make love after lunch.'

She said teasingly, 'I thought this was going to be a weekend of healthy outdoor pursuits . . . canoeing, that sort of thing.'

'The outdoor sports come later. This weekend indoor games have priority. Have some more champagne.'

They finished the meal by sharing a cantaloup melon with a generous measure of almond liqueur in the hollows where the seeds had been. With the coffee he produced some delicious dark handmade chocolates.

'I have a feeling you've spent too much of your life disciplining your senses instead of indulging them,' he said, selecting a chocolate and putting it into her mouth where it proved to be filled with delicious mocha fondant.

Presently they cleared the table, putting the dishes in the dishwasher to be dealt with later.

'Siesta time,' said Laurier, when the tidying away was completed.

He slipped his arm round her waist and steered her back to the bedroom.

'I must brush my teeth,' she said as, for the second time that day, he locked the door.

'Me, too. Is that something you like to do privately or can we do it together?'

'Why not?'

In the bathroom he said, 'You don't want to get toothpaste on your robe. I should take it off.'

He was standing behind her as he spoke and his arms went round her to unfasten the sash and draw the robe open. The loose sleeves slipped easily down her arms. Having hung the robe on the hook on the back of the door, he put his arms round her again, stroking her smooth bare midriff, looking over the top of her head at her round rose-tipped breasts.

His hands rose higher. 'They're so soft,' he murmured. 'Everything about you is lovely, but especially these.'

To see his strong hands caressing her in the mirror intensified the still unfamiliar thrill of his touch. She leaned back against the solid wall of his chest and watched, through her lowered lashes, the long fingers gently playing with her.

A *frisson* of exquisite feeling feathered down her spine. She found herself purring with enjoyment, rubbing her shoulders against him, her spine curving to thrust her breasts against the warmth of his palms.

Laurier lowered his head to press his lips to her shoulder from the top of her arm to her neck, meanwhile nudging her closer to the basin until she was trapped between the counter surrounding it and the tall male body behind her.

Alex's head drooped forward as his lips travelled over her nape and the top of her spine. He began, very lightly, to bite her, making her muffle a groan not of pain but of pleasure. She hadn't known how good it would be to feel the touch of his teeth there.

Lower down, at the base of her spine, she could feel him hardening against the soft cleft of her buttocks.

With an effort she lifted her head. 'We're supposed to be brushing our teeth,' she said hoarsely, looking at the reflection of her flushed cheeks and bright, excited eyes. It was the first time she had seen herself like this—a woman hungry for love.

His hold on her slackened enough for her to squirm round to face him and begin unbuttoning his shirt, a task prolonged by the shakiness of her hands. She had to tug the bottom of it out of his trousers before she could push it off his shoulders and run her palms over his chest.

The first time they had been naked together, that morning, she had been vaguely aware that he wasn't a hairy man. Now she saw, and it pleased her, that his chest was as smooth as polished hide. Her fingers explored the planes formed by the underlying muscles with as much tactile pleasure as he had derived from feeling her contrasting softness.

'You forgot to unbutton my cuffs,' he pointed out.

'Oh ... so I did.'

Quickly she remedied the oversight and he let the shirt fall to the floor.

Her cream silk pyjamas were held at the waist by shirring. He stretched the elastic, eased it down past her hips and the silk formed a pool round her feet. This time it was he who gave a kind of strangled groan before snatching her against him and bringing his mouth down on hers.

Presently he picked her up and carried her through to the bedroom where he lowered her on to the bed and then rapidly stepped out of his Topsiders and stripped off his trousers. He was not wearing underwear or socks. As he stretched himself beside her, she saw that the whole of his body, including his feet and his loins, was the same deep golden-brown. There must be a beach in Hawaii where he could lie naked in the sun after surfing.

She didn't want to think about Hawaii or about London, their bases. This island, this room, this bed, was where they belonged for the present.

As his fingertips stroked her cheek and then slipped down her throat to her breast, Alex closed her eyes and gave a luxurious sigh.

In the night, she woke up to find the room full of moonlight and Laurier leaning over her, his hand warm and strong and sure at the top of her thighs.

When he saw her eyes open, he put his lips close to her ear and said, in a husky murmur, 'I want you, Alex.'

'I want you,' she whispered back, putting her arms round him, opening her legs, inviting immediate possession.

'Uh-uh.' The soft North American negative was followed by feather-light kisses along the line of her jaw. 'Soon ... but not yet.' His lips arrived at her mouth, hovering with tantalising lightness, his own desire held in check while he drove her almost to the point of losing control.

Time and again, when she was on the brink of that final wild flood of feeling, he withheld the ultimate rapture; and each time the pleasure she felt was more overwhelming.

'Oh God, I can't stand it,' she muttered; her body writhing and trembling with rapturous sensation as his mouth and hands taught her responses she hadn't known she had in her.

Laurier let her rest for a moment, his dark eyes burning and hungry in the silvery twilight. It amazed her that he could control his passion for so long.

Suddenly he rolled on to his back, pulling her with him and holding her above him to nuzzle the globes of her breasts. She knelt astride him, all inhibitions swept away as his mouth feasted on her soft flesh. It seemed to her then that the whole purpose of her existence was to let him enjoy her body and to enjoy his caresses.

It was dawn before they went to sleep in each other's arms. When they woke up and disentangled themselves, the angle of the sunlight making the water shimmer indicated that it must be several hours later than their usual meeting time on the sea wall.

'Vancouver seems a million miles away,' said Alex, stretching. 'I feel wonderful,' she added, throwing back the covers and bouncing out of bed.

'I feel pretty good, too,' he agreed, swinging long legs over the edge of the mattress.

With tousled hair and dark stubble accentuating the hard exciting cut of his jaw and outlining the passionate mouth which had driven her wild a few hours ago, he had a slightly raffish air which she found even more attractive than his usual well-groomed appearance.

'You go take a shower. I'll get the kettle on.'

She was still in the shower, massaging conditioner into her wet hair, when he opened the sliding glass door.

'Mind if I join you?'

'Please do. I have to leave this stuff on my hair for a minute or two.'

He adjusted the rose so that the spray wouldn't hit her and turned on the water. Standing at the back of the spacious compartment, watching him lather himself, she remembered the first time she had seen that powerful back, never dreaming that less than a month later she would be sharing a shower with him.

'Ready to rinse now?' he asked, an outstretched arm inviting her to join him under the jet of warm water.

She nodded and moved towards him. Laurier's arm closed round her and drew her close. They kissed, slowly and with relish.

'Forget breakfast, let's make it brunch,' he said, when he turned off the water.

A few minutes later, towels spread over the pillows, they were back in bed, making love again.

That night, after dark, he introduced her to shallow-water shrimping. As clouds had blown up during the afternoon and there was no moonlight, he insisted on her wearing a life-jacket in case she should fall off the jetty where the operation took place. To her surprise, the equipment needed included a small camp stove for cooking their catch on the spot.

'We could take them up to the cottage but half the fun of the thing is cooking them right on the wharf by flashlight,' he explained, after showing her the simple home-made trap used for catching the little crustaceans.

This consisted of a metal hoop with a piece of old burlap

sewn to it, forming a basket, and four wires attached to the rim and converging above the centre of the sacking where they were joined to a long line.

As well as the precautionary life-jacket, he made her put on some old clothes left at the cottage by one of his teenage nieces.

'No sense in spoiling your good things. Susie won't mind,' he assured her.

So Alex went down to the dock in borrowed jeans with a sweater of his over Susie's shirt because it was one of those nights when soon after sunset the temperature had dropped by several degrees. She would have been cold without the big oiled-wool sweater enveloping her.

The bait was a can of sardines punched full of holes.

'A ripe fish head is the best bait but this should do the trick,' he remarked, as he lowered the trap into the water and secured the line.

He had brought down a couple of camp stools. They sat in the dark—which actually wasn't total darkness when the eyes became accustomed to it—listening to the wash of the water round the pilings beneath them, the only soft sound in the silence.

Presently Laurier reached for her hand and spent a few moments pressing soft kisses on her knuckles.

'You don't dislike being out here at night, do you?' he asked.

'What a strange thing to ask. Why should I dislike it?'

'Some people find it scary to be in an isolated place with no other houses nearby. It's a bit like the edge of the world out here.'

By 'people' did he mean some other girl who had come here with him? She pushed the thought out of her mind.

'I might not enjoy being alone here, but as long as you're with me I like it,' she answered. 'Are there any bears on the larger islands?'

'Not any more. I once met some campers from Europe

who'd been woken up in the night by a noise which had had them worried until they discovered they were listening to sea lions pillow-talking.' His laugh echoed over the water. 'In June and July the northern sea lions mate in shallow bays around the islands. One bull will have up to twenty cows. If you see them together from a distance they can look like a small log boom. I've never seen any around here, but we've often had harbour seals sunbathing on our beach.'

'Why are the islands called the Gulf Islands when, on the map, the passage between Vancouver Island and the mainland is shown as the Georgia Strait?' she asked.

'Originally the passage was named by Captain Vancouver of the Royal Navy. He called it the Gulf of Georgia in honour of King George the Third. About eighty years later it was re-named by an admiral, but Vancouver's name for it stuck.'

He let go of her hand to stand up and shine the flashlight into the depths.

'Nothing doing so far. Sometimes, when the shrimp start biting, you can haul up three or four full traps in less than an hour. Then there'll be a lull for a while before the next wave shows up.'

In the darkness, Alex sat thinking about the settlers who had come to this northwest corner of the Pacific rim long ago to make their homes and raise children here. What courage it must have taken for a bride to leave her homeland and everything familiar to share her husband's struggle to tame their small patch of wilderness. Yet, for all they had had to endure in the way of physical hardships and primitive living conditions, in some ways life for a woman must have been less complex and difficult than it was now.

For most of them marriage had been the only option. A few, very few, had done something else with their lives. But in general their destinies had been determined for them. Some might have resented conforming to the pattern,

particularly the enforced child-bearing during their fertile
years. Yet even though women in western countries were
free of that burden now, they still weren't free of the
emotional conditioning which told them that not to have
children was to miss out on life's most important
experiences.

Here on the island she was very much aware of that
emotional pressure. The cottage was full of reminders that
it wasn't normally a hideaway for lovers but a family place.
There were children's books on the shelves and children's
life-jackets and rubber boots in the utility room. The
growth rate of all Laurier's nephews and nieces was marked
on one of the living-room walls. Photographs of island
birthday parties, of teenage boys and girls proudly holding
up salmon they had caught and of smaller children
expertly paddling canoes or crewing in sailing boats
decorated other walls.

Yet reason and memory told Alex that family life, even
on holiday, was not all loving co-operation and laughter.
Outbreaks of squabbling and sulks also occurred, and even
when everyone was happy there was seldom much time for
the mother of the family to relax.

When had her aunt, once a talented artist, ever had a
chance to paint without interruption? Never. She had
always been too busy fulfilling her role as universal
provider of everything from snacks to first aid.

As soon as a woman had children she was on call twenty-
four hours a day. Even if she could afford to pay people to
relieve her of some of her maternal responsibilities, usually
she was nagged by guilt that she wasn't being a proper
mother and her children would suffer from her neglect.

'You're very quiet,' said Laurier.

Unwilling to share her thoughts with him, she said,
'Doesn't talking put the shrimps off?'

For answer he shone the flashlight again and asked her to
hold it for him while he slowly pulled up the trap. As it

came near the surface of the water she saw dozens of small shining beads which proved to be the eyes of the shrimps clustering round the bait.

'These are coon-stripes,' he told her, tipping them into a bucket of salt water and lowering the trap again. 'Some people rinse them in fresh water, but that spoils the flavour. They taste best if they're boiled in seawater with some extra salt added. But we'll catch some more before we start cooking.

Up to that point she hadn't given any thought to the manner of the shrimps' demise. Now, realising the creatures were soon to be boiled, she wondered if she could enjoy eating them. To buy dead shrimps from a fishmonger was different from being a witness to their execution. However, she knew it was unrealistic to eat things which other people had killed but to jib at being a party to the death of Laurier's catch.

If she mentioned her qualms, he would think her a fool. He was a kind man, a gentle man. But he was also a realist who might respect a vegetarian's views but would be justifiably impatient of inconsistent scruples.

After the second catch the shrimps were cooked for a few minutes, which turned them red, and then drained and given time to cool. When they were ready to eat, he showed her how to break off the head and press the tail, forcing the meat out of the shell.

Dipped in a special sauce made by one of his sisters-in-law, a pot of which he had brought to the island with him, the shrimps were delicious. There was a bottle of white wine to drink with them, and some garlic bread which, well wrapped, was still warm from the oven.

'Mm . . . a feast for the gods,' Alex murmured presently.

'Maybe not a feast, but a pretty good appetiser,' said Laurier.

In the subdued light of the fixed beam of the flashlight, he put a peeled shrimp on the paper plate on her lap. He was faster and more expert at dealing with them than she was. Of every two he peeled, he gave one to her.

Although, in this instance, he was just being nice, she felt sure he was a man who, if he were ever in circumstances when food was in short supply, would be equally generous.

'That's deliberate. These things are an aphrodisiac,' he told her, with a teasing grin, when she protested that she was having more than he.

'I know oysters are supposed to be. I didn't know these were.'

'Not if they're frozen. But fresh shrimp straight out of the sea—oh, yes!' he said, rolling his eyes.

She laughed. 'Are you implying that you're finding me an unexciting companion and hope the shrimps will ginger me up?'

In the act of raising his glass, he checked the movement, his amused expression becoming serious.

'Until we came here I wasn't sure how we'd get on in bed. I knew how much I wanted you, but I felt it might not work out. There was a reserve about you, a kind of coldness which puzzled me. That one kiss, when I managed to break through the ice for a few minutes, wasn't a lot to go on.'

He paused. 'But now I know my instinct was right. The reserve is only a façade. The real Alexandra is warm ... sexy ... fun to be with, in bed and out.'

This said, he continued the interrupted act of drinking. Above the rim of the glass, his dark eyes added a postscript that it wouldn't be long before they made love again.

She felt quite overcome by his tribute. Happiness welled up inside her. In that instant she felt that nothing in life mattered more than to live with and be loved by this rare and wonderful man whom fate had been keeping in store for her.

She gave him a glowing smile. Words of love trembled on her tongue. But she only allowed herself to say, in a light tone, 'That must be because you're a very good lover,

Laurier. Perhaps it's the French blood in you. In fact, I'm beginning to believe that the myth about Frenchmen has some foundation.'

They had left a pizza in the oven and a salad in the refrigerator to complete their supper. But when they returned to the cottage, he said, 'We'll eat later ... hm?' and left the pizza cooling on the worktop while he swept her off to the bedroom.

Waking up, Alex discovered that the clouds had gone and now the view from the window was bathed in bright moonlight. She wondered what time it was.

When Laurier had undressed her, he hadn't removed her watch, but her left arm was under the pillow. She doubted if she could move it without disturbing him. Time by the clock wasn't important. It was night and she was in bed with her lover's arm round her. That was all she needed to know.

Remembering her total abandonment, she thought it had been the wine rather than the shrimps which had swept away the last of her inhibitions. She hadn't known it was in her to respond like that. It could never have happened with Peter, but with Laurier making love had new dimensions.

Next morning, before they got up, he said, 'Do you have any unbreakable engagements today? Could we postpone going back for twenty-four hours?'

Her spirits soared. 'I ought not to, but—yes. Why not?' she answered recklessly.

'We'll still leave here right after breakfast but we'll head for Victoria and have a night there. How does that idea appeal?'

Alex would have preferred to stay on the island but sensed that he thought he would be giving her a treat by taking her to see the capital of British Columbia.

After breakfast, she said, 'Won't there be a problem

finding somewhere to stay without a reservation during Thanksgiving week?'

'I don't think so. If there is, we can always come back here. The most famous hotel in Victoria is the old Empress, but it's seen better days. I prefer Laurel Point Inn. We'll try for a room there.'

'All right, but let it be my treat. I've contributed nothing so far.'

He shook his head. 'I invited you—remember?'

'Yes, but going to Victoria is an extra. Why should you foot all the bills? It isn't fair.'

'It's the way I like it.' He grinned at her. 'When an irresistible feminist like you meets an old-fashioned sexist like me ... something's gotta give, kiddo.'

The joking rejoinder was an allusion to part of a recording of golden oldies they had played during their stay on the island.

'At least let me take you out to dinner tonight,' she persisted.

'Definitely not. Save those equal rights gestures for colleagues. We're not in that kind of relationship.'

Was he as aware as she of the question which was the natural corollary to that statement.

What kind of relationship are we in?

CHAPTER FOUR

'WE'RE not equals?' Alex said, raising her eyebrows in a playful pretence of being ready to take umbrage.

'You know we're not. I'm stronger than you are.'

Laurier demonstrated by taking her wrists in a firm clasp, pinning them behind her and pulling her against him.

She had to lean back to look into his mocking dark eyes. She said, 'But you wouldn't really use your strength against me.'

'Are you sure?'

'Completely.'

'But you can't get away unless I let you. Doesn't that bother you?'

'It would—if I wanted to get away,' Alex said, in a soft sexy murmur, pressing her hips closer. As he let go of her wrists to embrace her, she wrenched free and darted away. The flight and pursuit which followed could have ended sooner but it pleased him to let her elude him for a few minutes.

The Laurel Point Inn was a modern low-rise hotel built on a peninsula between the inner and outer harbours and surrounded by public gardens sloping down to the water's edge. It was close to the heart of the city yet secluded from traffic and bustle.

'After three days on the island I'm ready to stretch my legs. Do you feel like a walk?' he asked, when they had been shown to their room and were standing on the balcony, looking at their view.

'Yes, I do,' she agreed. 'I'm sure I've put on several pounds since we left Vancouver.'

He put his arm round her. The gardens below were deserted. There was no one to see him slide a caressing hand from her breast to her thigh.

'If you have, it's only an improvement. You're in beautiful shape.'

'Thank you, but I don't think either of us would stay in shape if we ate and drank and lazed around like this all the time. I expect what you'd really enjoy is a run, isn't it?'

'Later, maybe. Right now I have a better idea.'

He didn't say what it was, but she could read it in his eyes.

Stroking her had aroused him, as it had her. Although they had made love after breakfast, already they wanted to repeat the pleasure.

Half an hour later, lying in his arms, her eyes closed, she thought, now that I've had this, how am I going to get through the rest of my life without it? I was better off before, not knowing what it could be like with a lover as wonderful as he is. Never doing this again will be like never hearing music, never drinking wine, never lying in the sun or in a warm, scented bath.

If only we lived somewhere near each other. If only he didn't have to go back to Hawaii and I didn't have to go back to London ...

Believing her to be sleeping, Laurier began to ease carefully away. Alex didn't open her eyes. She was afraid that if she did he would see something in them which betrayed that her thoughts were not appropriate to the happy aftermath of love.

She heard him go into the bathroom and close the door quietly behind him. She rolled over, burying her face in the pillow. But she couldn't give vent to the despair which overwhelmed her. Laurier was too observant to miss any visible signs that all was not well. Besides, to think about the future was to mar the present. To anticipate unhappiness was negative. The positive attitude was to count herself lucky to have this extra day and night with him. And even tomorrow would not be the end. They would see each other again. They might even spend some more nights together. Mrs Tait didn't wait up for her grandson to come home at night, and he always left the house very early, before she was awake. Unless some emergency occurred in the small hours, she wouldn't know Laurier had been out all night.

I won't think about the end of it, Alex resolved, sitting up and finger-combing her tousled hair.

When Laurier returned to the bedroom, she had turned on the radio and was humming as she straightened the bed.

The heart of the capital was dominated by the green-domed Parliament buildings facing north across the inner harbour and the creeper-clad, château-style bulk of the Empress Hotel, facing west. In spite of the rival grandeur of these two edifices, the city lacked the bustle and sophistication of Vancouver; it reminded Alex of resorts on the south coast of England. After a light lunch in the hotel, she and Laurier had only to walk a few blocks to reach the sea and a pleasant path across grassy public land.

'This is Juan de Fuca Strait, which runs into the Pacific. The land over there is America,' he explained, indicating the hazy outlines of distant mountains.

As they started to step out more briskly, he reached for her hand and held it loosely in his as they swung along the path, not walking as fast as she did in the mornings on the sea wall but still covering the ground much more swiftly than most people out for a stroll in the November sun.

As the paths of a large pleasant park led them back in the direction of the city, Laurier said, 'I don't think you're going to find the shops here anything to rave about, but you might like to look at the Emily Carr gallery. I know you're interested in her.'

Emily Carr was one of two Canadian women, both long dead, whose lives fascinated Alex. She had first heard of Emily Carr in the gallery named after her in Vancouver Art Gallery. The other Canadian, Pauline Johnson, whose grave was among the trees in Stanley Park, had been mentioned to her by Laurier's grandmother.

What Carr and Johnson had in common was that, born in 1871 and 1862, an era when, particularly in Canada, it wasn't easy for women to live independent lives, they had both been free spirits, driven by a need to express themselves in their own way.

Emily Carr, named Klee Wyck, Laughing One, by the Nootka Indians among whom one of her sisters had trained as a missionary, had died in Victoria in 1945, leaving a heritage of powerful, mysterious paintings completely unlike the pretty amateurish watercolours produced by most artistic women of her period.

The gallery, though small, gave Alex some further insights into the character of the woman whose genius had driven her to leave Victoria to study in San Francisco, England and France. As she signed her name in the visitors' book, she wondered if Emily Carr had confronted the choice which faced Alex, the choice between a man she loved and the work she loved.

From the gallery they wandered through the main shopping streets and she kept an eye open for presents for her cousins.

'Cowichan Indian sweaters are the thing most tourists buy here,' Laurier told her. 'I don't like them myself, but maybe you will. The Cowichans were taught to knit by the mission-
aries. Before that they wove blankets, using wool which mountain goats left on bushes and sometimes scraps of coloured cloth given them by the fur traders. I think the blankets were probably a lot more interesting than the sweaters.'

When she saw the heavy sweaters made from coarse undyed oiled wool in shades of black, white and grey, with horizontal bands of pattern, Alex agreed with him. The workmanship was crude compared with the fine basketry they had admired in the museum in Vancouver.

* * *

The hotel had a covered swimming-pool and also a whirlpool which they had to themselves. The tall windows by the whirlpool faced west. As they sat with the sun on their faces and the warm water churning and frothing, Laurier said, 'Can I tempt you to play hookey for one more day? I'd like to show you the Comox Valley. There's some great scenery up there.'

Her heart ached with longing to say yes, but she knew she mustn't.

'I'd like to see it, but not tomorrow,' she answered regretfully. 'I must get back to work. I'm up to schedule at present, but that could change if unforeseen snags arise. When we go up to the room, I'd better call my hotel and check if there've been any messages for me. Getting back to people the same day, if it's humanly possible, is one of my basic principles.'

'OK, you do that,' he agreed. 'But if there haven't been calls for you, I don't see that twenty-four hours can make all that difference. You know the old saying about all work and no play.'

If only he knew how hard it was to resist.

'I've just had three days' wonderful play,' she said lightly. 'And that old saying doesn't apply to people like you and me who enjoy what we do for a living. My work is a permanent holiday compared with most people's lives. I'm never bored for a minute. I don't suppose you are either. We're two very lucky people.'

They had dinner at a restaurant originally built as a private house for a prosperous family in the last century. Wood-panelled walls, the soft glow of oil lamps, dark red bobble-trimmed velvet curtains and waitresses dressed as parlourmaids in starched aprons with bibs and streamers over black dresses enhanced the old-world atmosphere.

Soon after their arrival, a couple in their early twenties were shown to a table nearby.

'Honeymooners, wouldn't you say?' Laurier murmured,

a few minutes later.

Alex nodded. 'From a very small town where the only place to eat out is a fast-food diner.'

There was nothing patronising in her remark. She was touched by the signs that, to the bride and her young husband, a city the size of Victoria and a restaurant with damask tablecloths, real flowers and long-stemmed glasses was the height of sophistication. She could remember her own excitement and nervousness the first time she had dined at an elegant restaurant in London, although it had in fact been a good deal more awe-inspiring than this one.

'They're much too young to be married, of course. That girl can't have any idea what life might have had to offer if she hadn't chosen the very first thing on the menu,' she added, with a feeling of mingled envy and pity for the starry-eyed bride who was proudly watching her husband studying the wine list.

Probably he knew as little about wine as she did, but they both felt it was his prerogative to decide what they would drink.

'Were you never tempted to do that?' Laurier asked.

They were sharing a corner banquette upholstered with crimson plush. A wall lamp above and behind him gave his dark hair an ebony sheen.

'No, fortunately not. When I was in my teens, one of my cousins rushed into marriage too young, so that was an early object lesson. When I went to art school in London, it wasn't marriage the male students had in mind. So, as you did, I got through the worst danger zone and had time to finish growing up—which they haven't,' she added, nodding at the younger couple.

'It may work out. Sometimes it does. I have a friend who married when he was in college. They're still two happy people who haven't changed their minds about each other.'

'Perhaps they knew who they were very early in life. A few people grow up faster than the majority.'

Marriage wasn't a subject she wanted to dwell on. To

steer the conversation into a less dangerous channel, she asked what he thought of a large oil painting hanging on the far side of the restaurant.

The Parliament buildings were outlined by hundreds of electric lights and the façade of the Empress was floodlit when, later, they strolled round the harbour before returning to Laurel Point.

Their room was on the third floor, with a balcony overlooking the water. It had a grass-green carpet, a chevron-patterned quilted cover on the wide double bed and three pictures of birds grouped in a row above the headboard.

Alex shrugged off her black cashmere jacket and put it on a hanger in the wardrobe.

When she turned, Laurier was close behind her. He took hold of her hands.

'When you get to my age, you don't rush into saying "I love you" until you're sure of your feelings. This weekend has proved to me that I want to spend the rest of my life with you. I believe you feel the same way. Am I right?'

She wanted, desperately, to fling her arms round him and say, 'Darling Laurier—yes! You know you are.'

Instead she looked at him in silence, her throat constricted, her mouth dry.

'What's the matter?' he asked, after a moment. 'It can't be much of a surprise. The only thing we haven't done this weekend is to put into words how we feel about each other. But we've exchanged pretty clear signals in all the other forms of communication.'

He was smiling at her as he spoke, his eyes full of loving tenderness.

Alex felt literally petrified. She couldn't move. She couldn't speak. She had disciplined herself against day-dreaming of this wonderful, terrible possibility. Now it had arisen, she had no idea how to handle it.

It was only when he moved closer, intending to take her in his arms, that she regained enough control to step back a pace and say urgently, 'No . . . please . . . wait a minute. This *is* a surprise to me . . . and we can't spend our lives together.'

'Why not? Certainly we can. After this, I can't live without you,' he told her, recapturing her hands. 'I love you, Alexandra. I thought I was never going to find a woman who made me feel this way. It's much more than being "in love". It's wanting to share a whole house, not only a bed, with you. It's wanting to have children with you.'

She attempted to withdraw her hands, but he wouldn't release them.

'But I can't give you children,' she burst out, trying to pull free.

'You mean you can't have them?' he asked. 'Are you sure? How do you know?' Before she could answer, he went on, 'Is that what's been on your mind? I know there's been something bothering you.'

She bit her lip. 'Perhaps . . . in a way . . . but——'

He broke into her faltering explanation, saying, 'My poor little love, has it made you very unhappy? But it doesn't prevent us being parents. We can adopt a family. You told me your aunt and uncle were as fond of their adopted children as they were of their natural offspring. We shall feel the same way about ours.'

That he had reacted with tender concern for her feelings, rather than showing either shock or disappointment on his own account, didn't make it any easier to say, 'You don't understand. As far as I know there isn't any physical reason why I can't have children. I don't want to have them. I—I made that decision some years ago.'

He was visibly baffled. 'Why?'

She took advantage of his slackened grasp to free her hands and step away from him.

She cleared her throat and took a deep breath to compose herself. 'Because I know I can't cope with being a designer *and* a wife and mother, and I want to go on being a designer. My career is very important to me—as important as yours is to you. I want to give it all my time and energy, which wouldn't be possible if I had children and a husband.'

There was a short, tense pause before he said, 'Are you telling me you don't want to get married?'

She nodded. 'There's no way I can run two careers—and being a wife *is* a career, and a very demanding one. If I were going to have children I should want to bring them up properly, giving them most of my time, especially when they were small. Maybe I don't have very strong maternal instincts, but I would rather devote all my time and energy to being a designer.'

Slowly Laurier's eyebrows became a dark bar across his forehead and she watched his look of bewilderment change to an angry glare.

'Then what in hell's name are you doing here with me this weekend?' he demanded explosively.

She flinched. 'I—I didn't know you were going to ask me to marry you.

'You thought it was a three-night stand? Like hell you did!' he said furiously. 'You wouldn't have come if you'd thought that. You knew I was serious about you. Didn't you?' With two strides he closed the space between them and seized hold of her. 'Didn't you?'

'You're hurting me,' she protested, as his long powerful fingers pressed the soft flesh of her upper arms.

'Do you think it doesn't hurt to tell a girl you love her and be told that her career is more important?' he snapped back. But the bite of his fingers eased slightly, although he didn't let go.

She said in a low, controlled tone, 'Don't lose your temper, Laurier. Think about it for a minute. Could you contemplate giving up oceanography for me? I could afford to support you in reasonable comfort. Would you run our home and bring up our children? Would *you* relegate *your* career to something of secondary importance?'

The suggestion threw him.

'Like hell you would,' she said quietly, in an ironic echo of his own rebuttal.

To his credit, he didn't come back with the argument, blunt or implied, that because he was a man his career was more important than hers. She was spared the disappointment of finding that, under a veneer of enlightened attitudes, there lurked a hard core of sexism.

His hands slid down her arms to recapture her hands. 'No, but I'd do my best to share the domestic responsibilities with you. I'm not asking you to cook and clean for me. As my wife you'd have fewer chores than you have at present. We would have some staff to look after us and our children.'

'That's easily said but not so easily achieved. Reliable housekeepers and nannies are difficult to find. But even if they weren't, that isn't the major obstacle. The main reason why I can't marry is because I don't work in one city or even one country. My practice is international. I don't want to turn down commissions because they happen to be on the other side of the world and may take several months to complete. I need to enlarge my professional horizons, not contract them. How would you react to that—a wife who wasn't around for weeks at a time? I don't think it would work. I know it wouldn't.'

He had heard her out in frowning silence. She had never seen him look so grim. The lips which normally had a humorous slant were now tightly compressed. After a brief lull, his dark eyes were angry again.

'My God, you liberated women accuse us of lousy behaviour but you're no better than we are!' he blazed at her. 'If I were saying these things to you, when you'd thought I had marriage in mind, I'd be the rat of the year. But reverse the situation and that's different. Women mustn't be treated as sex objects, but to use a man as a stud is perfectly OK.'

'That isn't fair,' she protested. 'When I agreed to this weekend I didn't know that your intentions were serious. I only knew how *I* felt . . . that I liked you enough to ignore all the usual reasons why I don't go in for lovers.' His increasingly crushing grip on her fingers made her wince. 'You're hurting me again.'

He released her hands as if they were suddenly red-hot.

'I thought you were the kind of woman who would only go to bed for love,' he retorted harshly.

She hesitated, uncertain whether an admission of the extent of her feelings would make matters better or worse.

She watched him pace round the room with long restless strides, his hands thrust into his pockets, every line of his posture indicative of repressed rage.

She decided she owed him the truth. 'I am. I do love you, Laurier.' As he stopped short and swung to face her, she added sadly, 'But not enough to sacrifice my work and the reputation I'm building. I can't give that up any more than you can give up yours. It's not fair to ask me.'

'Was it fair to let me fall in love with you, knowing you had no intention of becoming my wife?'

'I didn't know you were in danger of loving me. An attractive man who's still single at your age can't be too susceptible.'

He was silent, glowering at her.

She said, 'Nowadays men and women go away together all the time. Usually it has no special significance. It's just . . . an enjoyable thing to do. I—I loved you enough to think a few days together would be worth whatever it cost me. But I had no way of knowing it would hurt you when we parted. How could I know that? You never hinted you were serious.'

'I should think the fact that I didn't try to rush you into bed should have indicated that my interest was more than casual,' he said acidly.

'Not conclusively. What would you have had me do? Tell you, right at the outset, that I didn't intend to get married? Be fair about it, Laurier, how could I do that? Men don't announce their intentions right at the outset, and nor can women.'

'When I asked you to come to the island with me, you could have made it clear then. If I had had nothing in mind but sex with no strings, I'd have made sure you understood that.'

She said, 'I thought that was probably just what you did have in mind. I knew I was going to get hurt and I decided it was worth it. I'm sorry you're being hurt too—truly I am. You're the last person in the world I would hurt if it could be avoided. I—I should have stuck to my guns and not seen you after that first date. My instinct told me we shouldn't go on seeing each other; but I thought the only danger was to myself . . . to my feelings.'

His mouth was hard, his eyes hostile. 'So you say now, but perhaps what your instinct told you was that I shouldn't like being made a fool of.'

As he spoke, he strode to the door.

'Where are you going?' she exclaimed.

'I don't know, but I'm not sleeping here. If you want a man in your bed tonight you'll have to find someone else. Try the bar downstairs,' he said brutally.

Seconds later the door slammed behind him.

Alex collapsed on the side of the bed, her whole body shaking with shock. In less than five minutes they had changed from lovers to enemies. She could understand Laurier's fury. It was much more her fault than his that things had come to this pass.

For the first time in many years—indeed since the unhappy months after the death of her parents—she burst into tears.

It was almost two in the morning and, with the curtains drawn back, she was lying awake, her eyes swollen and sore from much weeping, when she heard the outer door open.

Laurier had left the key in the room. Because in her anguished state of mind it didn't occur to her immediately that he could have asked for another key, she thought for a moment it was someone else coming in. Alarmed, she reached for the light switch, prepared to snatch up the telephone, hoping the night porter wasn't far from the switchboard.

When she saw who it was, she was relieved, not only because it was not an intruder, but because she had spent hours worrying that Laurier might do something foolish like getting himself smashed and then trying to fly the float-plane back to the island or Vancouver.

As soon as she saw his face, she knew she ought to have known he wasn't the type to react to a bad situation by drinking too much. He looked very tired, but quite sober.

He came to the foot of the bed and stared at her in silence for a moment. When her outburst of weeping had died down, Alex had washed her face. Although she had spent some time holding a face cloth, soaked in cold water and wrung out, over her eyes, it was impossible for even several cold compresses to restore her eyelids to normal. Only time would do that.

'I'm sorry,' he said, in a quiet voice. 'I had no right to insult you. I lost my temper. Forgive me.'

'Oh, Laurier——'

She had thought she had no tears left but suddenly her gaze was blurred, her mouth quivering uncontrollably.

He came round the bed in two strides, sat down and gathered her close.

'Don't cry. For God's sake, don't cry. I didn't mean any of those rotten things I said to you. We'll work something out . . . we have to.'

Alex hadn't the strength then to tell him there was no way to resolve the conflict between their feelings and their incompatible careers. She was too emotionally strung up to be capable of explaining that to him, convincing him. She knew it was madness to let him hold her and comfort her, but she couldn't help herself.

With her face buried against his shoulder and her slim body heaving with sobs, she wept for the happy future which, in a different era, they might have spent together.

Laurier patted and soothed her as if she were a small child. He stroked her thick streaky blonde hair, his hands gentle now. Presently, when she was calmer, he tipped up her tear-wet face and tenderly blotted her cheeks.

'You're worn out, my poor little love,' he said, as she sagged against him, too drained to care what her face must look like.

She knew she ought not to let him call her that. To weaken now would only make it harder to resist his persuasions tomorrow. But tonight she had been through too much agony of mind to have any willpower left.

He shook out her pillow and urged her to lie down.

'Try to get some sleep,' he suggested, stroking strands of damp hair away from her forehead.

She nodded and closed her eyes, only to open them again as he rose from the bed and began to take off his clothes.

'Where did you go?' she asked huskily.

He shrugged. 'I walked around . . . nowhere special. Go to sleep. We'll talk in the morning.' He switched on the light in the bathroom and then came back to put out the bedside light and leave her in semi-darkness.

Again Alex closed her eyes, but even though she was no longer racked by worry about his well-being her mind was not calm. She knew she had no hope of sleeping.

That Laurier was no longer angry had relieved her of the fear that her precious memories of the island would be spoiled by an acrimonious parting. At the same time, his new, kinder mood was going to make it much harder to stick to her guns. And it wasn't only his persuasion she had to fight. The greater part of her own nature was ranged against her. The longing for love and companionsip was a powerful force which had caused legions of women to surrender their ambitions. Could she stand fast against her instincts, her clamorous senses?

Had she been drowsy, she wouldn't have known Laurier had left the bathroom. He made no sound as he moved to his side of the bed but she saw his tall frame silhouetted against the window-wall for a moment and felt a slight movement of the mattress as he got into bed and stretched out beside her.

The thought of his naked body—she herself was wearing a nightdress—sent a tremor of longing through her. It was, she realised, her last chance to make love with him. After tonight there could be no question of seeing him again. Tomorrow they must say goodbye. But tonight, after so much pain—and with months of pain ahead—would it be wrong to experience the bliss of love just once more?

Aware that she was risking rejection—apart from the more complex reasons why he might not want her, he could be physically exhausted—but unable to control her longing, Alex moved a hand towards him.

For some seconds after her fingers touched the smooth warmth of his side there was no reaction. Could he have fallen asleep the instant his head touched the pillow?

She gasped as the still form beside her suddenly came to life and she found herself crushed in his arms, a shower of passionate kisses being rained all over her face.

Soon her nightdress was in the way. As she sat up and pulled it upwards, over her head, his hands found and covered her breasts while his lips burned a trail down her spine. She flung the nightdress away, her responses heightened by the knowledge that this was the last time.

In the morning she woke before he did. She had gone to sleep in his arms but now he was lying on his chest with his head turned towards her.

The sight of his sleeping face filled her with tenderness. He was everything she had ever hoped for in a man. How could she give him up? A man such as this—intelligent, kind, amusing and a brilliant lover—was as rare as a ten-carat diamond. Most women would think her crazy to contemplate saying goodbye to him.

But even today, with all the talk about equality, most women never experienced the intense satisfaction of building a career and enjoying real independence. Perhaps not as much as her mother's generation, but still very strongly, they were conditioned to feel that love was the reason for living, a prize worth any sacrifice.

Men didn't think that. Men didn't change their lifestyles, abandon their ambitions, renounce fame and fortune, or even more modest success, for love and fatherhood. A few had tried role-reversal but they were a tiny minority. It would be years, generations even, before there was any real balance between the careers of married couples. Even with unmarried partners it was still invariably the woman who made the greatest adjustments.

If I chafe at that now, in the abstract, I shall resent it much more when it's happening to me, she thought, leaning on her elbow to gaze at her love's closed eyelids and the humorous, sensual mouth which gave her such pleasure when it touched hers or kissed other parts of her body.

How lonely a single bed would seem after these nights of falling asleep in his arms. And yet her intelligence told her they couldn't go on for ever needing and wanting each other with the insatiable desire of the past few days. People never did. However wildly in love they were at the beginning, no one could live at this fever-pitch for a lifetime.

Hard as it was to imagine now, there must come a time when she and Laurier would go to bed wanting to read or to sleep rather than to make love. It was then, when their present consuming physical appetite for each other had subsided and taken its place among the rest of life's pleasures, that the destructive incompatibility of their occupations would make itself felt.

Yet even while she was trying to think sensibly and rationally, part of her was longing to wake him with loving caresses which would inevitably lead to a repetition of last night's passionate truce.

She was fighting the impulse to pull down the sheet which covered most of his broad brown back when Laurier stirred. A moment later his eyes opened.

'Hi,' he said drowsily, smiling at her. 'How long have you been awake?'

'Not long. I'll shower first, shall I?'

As she spoke, she turned on to her back and prepared to swing off the bed. As her toes touched the carpet, a long arm hooked round her waist and trapped her where she sat.

'We'll shower together—but not right now. We haven't said good morning properly.'

Hoisting himself into a sitting position and pulling her across his lap, he kissed her.

At first she hoped that if only she could remain passive he would be content with one kiss and then let her go. But the kiss went on for a long time. Long before their lips parted, her arms were wound round his neck and his hand was gentle on her breasts.

'We shouldn't ... we haven't time ...' was her faint unconvincing protest, when she could speak.

'I'll fly you back to Coal Harbour. From there it's only five minutes' walk to your place.'

Laurier spoke with his lips on her throat and his fingertips brushing lightly over her belly. Seconds later she gasped and her arms tightened round his neck as the first strong spasm of pleasure rippled outwards along every nerve in her body's rapid response to his sure, delicate touch.

Now there was no room in her mind for sensible thoughts, only joy that he could induce these wonderful, mind-blowing sensations which had for so long eluded her with a lover whose only concern had been his own gratification.

'I love you ... I need you, Alex,' he said huskily, close to her ear, when a few minutes later she lay dazed and panting, a fine dew glistening on her closed eyelids and forehead. 'We belong together.'

She opened her eyes, still bathed in the blissful aftermath of his caresses. 'I love you, too,' she whispered.

Then she started to make love to him until it was he who made smothered sounds through set teeth as, with soft hands and lips, she strove to give him the delight he had given her.

The long suntanned muscular torso rippled and quivered as she caressed the taut flesh of his chest and loins. His skin had a faint natural scent peculiar to him, she realised. It was as recognisable as the smell of a sun-ripened apple or a fine leather binding, but it wasn't common to all men. It was Laurier's scent, as individual as his fingerprints. She would never forget it. Or the springy, heathery texture of the dark curly hair at his groin. Or the heat and strength clasped in her hand which, when she traced his lips with the tip of her tongue, pulsed and throbbed even more strongly.

At last, with an explosive cry, he thrust her on to her back and sprang upon her, swiftly making them one with a deep groan of satisfaction as he plunged smoothly inside her.

Alex locked her long legs tightly round him. Their mouths fused in a kiss which went on and on. She wanted it never to end. She wanted to die in his arms.

Two hours later, by which time they were back in Vancouver, Laurier insisted on carrying her bag to the hotel before flying the float-plane back to its usual mooring.

As yet neither of them had made any reference to the angry scene of the night before. At breakfast they hadn't talked much at all.

As they neared the hotel, he said, 'When am I going to see you again?'

Throughout the return flight Alex had been wondering if he imagined that during the night or early this morning she had changed her mind. If so, she had to make it clear she had not. But not now. The street was no place for a conversation which might end in another flare-up.

'Why don't we meet for lunch at O'Douls?' she suggested.

In a restaurant they would have to keep their emotions under control.

'OK. One o'clock at O'Douls,' he agreed.

As always he saw her to the lift where he handed over the cabin bag.

'Thank you for a marvellous weekend, Laurier,' she said quietly. 'I shall never forget it as long as I live.' She spoke in a valedictory tone which she hoped would prepare him for what she must tell him at lunch.

His dark eyes looked down into hers and a faint smile touched his wide mouth. 'Nor I, my love,' he said softly, and brushed a light kiss on her cheek before turning away.

Although she had insisted on returning to work, Alex did nothing that morning. She found it impossible to think about anything but this appalling, heart-breaking dilemma to which there was no solution except the untenable one of sacrificing everything she had worked for.

Yet if she held fast to the career which meant so much to her, she must sacrifice all the joy and peace and fulfilment she had felt in his arms last night and again this morning. Not only that, but the warm companionship they had shared when they were not making love. Either way it was a ruinous choice which must leave them both incomplete.

O'Douls restaurant was a Vancouver landmark conveniently close to her hotel. Laurier was there before her, sitting at one of the tables overlooking the street. He rose as she came through the door and remained on his feet as she joined him.

They had both changed the clothes they had been wearing earlier. He was still casually dressed in a sports jacket over an open-necked shirt—O'Douls was an informal place catering to shoppers and tourists as well as businessmen. Deliberately, Alex had dressed to look like a career-woman attending a working lunch. She had clipped her blonde hair at her nape which added to the austere effect of a bow-tied black silk shirt under a grey cashmere blazer with a black and grey pleated plaid skirt. A string of matched pearls and pearl ear-studs and some shiny black bangles made the colours chic rather than funereal, but she could see Laurier wasn't taken by her transformation. As she walked towards him and his glance swept from her sleeked-back hair to her pewter-grey tights, she could tell that her outfit didn't meet with the approval he had given to the clothes she had worn on the day they set out for the island. Nevertheless he was smiling when she reached the table for two by the window.

'How was your grandmother's weekend?' she asked, as he drew out the other chair for her.

'She had a good time. She's hoping you'll come to dinner tonight, but I haven't committed you.'

'I'm glad you haven't, because I think I should work this evening, and turn in early to catch up some sleep,' she answered briskly, picking up the menu on her side of the table. 'Have you already decided what to eat?'

'No, but I ordered drinks. Mimosas. Is that OK?'

'I don't usually drink at lunchtime on working days, but I guess one mimosa won't hurt me. Here they come now,' she added, seeing a waitress approaching with two goblets on a tray.

As the girl was placing them on the table, Alex foresaw that Laurier might propose a toast which she couldn't, in honesty, drink to. To forestall him, she picked up her glass, saying, 'I've lunched here a couple of times and the atmosphere seems more French than Irish to me. Did I tell you I was hoping to fit in a couple of days in Montreal on my way back to Europe?'

Then, quickly, she took a sip of the mixture of champagne and orange juice.

'I believe you did mention it when we first knew each other.' Instead of tasting his mimosa, he put his right hand into the pocket of his jacket. To her acute dismay, he said,

'Why don't we go there together—as part of our honeymoon trip?'

Before she had recovered from the shock of this suggestion, he produced a small leather-covered box, opened it, and from the groove in the velvet lining extracted an emerald ring.

'This was left to me some years ago. I'd like you to wear it until we find something you like or maybe design your own engagement ring.'

Alex stared at the beautiful ring he was holding between his finger and thumb, a large square-cut emerald framed by diamonds.

A part of her longed to stretch out her hand and let him slide it on her finger. The ring symbolised so many of life's best gifts; companionship, tenderness, passion, mutual support. But wonderful as those things were, and much as she wanted to possess them, she knew they could only be had in exchange for the total freedom of her present lifestyle, the freedom to work at all hours, to go wherever her next commission took her and to stay there as long as was necessary.

The mere fact that Laurier was offering her the ring and speaking of honeymoon trips showed how little importance he had attached to the things she had told him last night. Clearly he didn't take her career as seriously as she did—as seriously as his own.

She swallowed the lump in her throat. 'It's beautiful . . . but you know I can't wear it . . . can't marry you. There's no way our lives can mesh.'

He leaned towards her, his dark gaze intent and burning. 'They have to. I can't give you up. I don't believe you can walk away from me, Alex. We're made for each other and you know it. Somehow we *have* to be together.'

'But we can't. It's just impossible. However much we care for each other, we can't ignore the difficulties . . . insurmountable difficulties. I'm not a young girl, filling in time between school and marriage with a job which doesn't

really matter to me. I'm a woman who's devoted years to a
lifetime career which gives me enormous satisfaction. I love
my work, Laurier. I can't give it up—not even for you.' Her
voice broke on the last few words and her eyes filled with
sudden tears.

At that moment the waitress returned to ask if they were
ready to order.

'Not yet. In a few minutes,' Laurier said, somewhat
curtly.

He had palmed the ring. Now he put it back in is pocket,
and the ring case after it. 'This is a hell of a place to have a
private conversation. Can't we go back to your place?'

'I'd rather not.' Alex opened the menu, although she had
never felt less like eating.

Scanning the list of dishes, forcing herself to concentrate,
she reached for her drink, hoping the champagne in it
would help her to pull herself together. As Laurier had said,
O'Douls was a most unsuitable place for a heart-to-heart of
this nature. But at least with a table between them, and an
audience of other lunchers, he couldn't take her in his arms
and coerce her with kisses and caresses.

'How about the avocado salad?' he suggested.

'Yes, that would be fine,' she agreed.

He signalled the waitress and ordered the salads and a
bottle of white wine. Then he took a long draught of his
mimosa, almost draining the glass before he replaced it on
the table and touched his napkin to his lips.

'I think maybe you don't realise what kind of place
Hawaii is,' he said, in a lighter tone than his impassioned
statement of a few minutes ago. 'On Oahu alone there are
many openings for designers. Honolulu is a growing city
and even though Waikiki is already teeming with hotels,
there is still room for more. Apart from offices and hotels,
there are condominiums and the large holiday houses built
on individual lots. You would never be short of work there.'

'Probably not,' she conceded.

During her sojourn in Florida, working on the commission which had been a contributory cause of the split with Peter, she had had her eyes opened to the difference between English and American attitudes to professional interior design.

In America the number of trained designers was, pro rata, much larger than in England. Even in towns of medium size, numerous designers were to be found listed in the Yellow Pages and in addition most department stores selling furnishings had design teams to advise customers on overall schemes.

This was not the case in England where only quite rich people employed professional designers and most people of moderate means relied on their own taste, with varying degrees of success.

In her opinion, the general standard of interior décor was higher in the United States than it was in her own country. But while America had many competent designers, it had few of outstanding brilliance. In London there were a number whose services were in demand all over the world and who ranked with the legendary John Fowler in the genius of their taste.

'I'm sure you're right. I could find plenty to do there, but that's not enough for me, Laurier. I've always aimed for the top. Although I may never get there, I can't stop trying. And to get to the top I have to be based in a capital city and I have to be able to travel. For the kind of commissions I want, Hawaii is too far off the beaten track. I couldn't function effectively from there, any more than you could function in the Mid-West.'

He was prevented from answering by the return of their waitress with the salads and the wine.

Not until she had left them, taking the empty mimosa goblets, did he say, 'Being famous won't make you happy.'

'It isn't the fame I want. It's the opportunities to create exciting interiors. Doing a succession of condos for retired North Americans might be profitable, but it wouldn't be as interesting as designing a penthouse here, a *palazzo* there.'

'You say Hawaii is off the beaten track, but in fact it's slap in the middle of all the Pacific Rim countries. You could pick up commissions in Australia, fly to Hong Kong and work for the Asian bankers who are now the world's richest men, or to Mexico where a lot of wealthy Americans have second homes in places like Acapulco and San Miguel Allende. There's just as much scope in and around the Pacific as there is in Europe and east coast America—and a helluva better climate,' he added, picking up his fork.

Alex followed suit but, instead of starting to eat, she said, 'I expect that's true, but I haven't any contacts there. My reputation isn't big enough yet for me to transplant myself without losing ground. This present job for John is an important springboard, but only in North America and the Caribbean. I don't think he has any plans to expand beyond the west coast.' She began to pick at her salad, wondering how she was ever going to get through it.

Whereas some people, when they were miserable, found comfort in eating, with Alex emotional upsets had the reverse effect and caused total loss of appetite. For weeks after the loss of her parents she had eaten so little that the Fishers had worried that she had developed a pre-teen form of anorexia nervosa. Their doctor, after talking to her, had assured them it was merely a reaction to shock which would eventually pass off, as indeed it had.

Now, torn between the man she loved and the passionate desire to realise her long-held ambitions, she found the lavish salad, usually her favourite food, completely unappetising, and regretted ordering it.

'I'm beginning to get the message that being under the aegis of this guy John is more important to you than the way I feel about you,' Laurier said curtly.

She looked up and saw that his lean face was taut and angry, as it had been the night he had demanded to know why she had brushed him off following their first dinner date.

This time he looked even fiercer, with a hostile gleam in

his eyes which made her say quickly, 'That's nonsense. I don't feel that at all, I assure you. And I'm not under his aegis. He's just a very useful contact through whom I may make other contacts, notably the people who stay in the Connaught Tower penthouse suites. You have absolutely no reason to be jealous of John Kassinopolis,' she added, perhaps unwisely.

He swallowed some wine and gave her a long brooding look. 'I'm beginning to wonder if I've been seeing straight,' he said, in a grim tone. 'They say love is blind. Maybe it is. Right up to last night when I asked you to marry me, I believed that you were a girl who would always put feelings first—other people's as well as your own. It seems I was wrong about that. It's not feelings which are important to you but things like success and fame and knowing the right people to help you achieve your ambitions.'

'Laurier, that isn't true,' she protested, stabbed by his tone. 'You know that's not all I care about. It isn't fair to accuse me of being unfeeling. It's precisely because I'm not that we're both in this mess. I—I let my feelings about you undermine my better judgement. I knew that falling in love could probably never work out for me, and I meant, and tried, to avoid it. I didn't want to hurt you. Surely you must realise that?'

Seeing her tormented expression, his angry look softened slightly.

'Then why go on doing it?' he asked. 'For God's sake, Alex, being a famous designer will be cold comfort when you're an older woman, not as beautiful as you are now, with no one to share your problems, let alone your bed. Have you thought how lonely your future will be in that empty bubble called fame?'

'Yes, I've thought about the future. And I've also looked around me and seen the numbers of women who got married too young and never fulfilled their potential, the women who stay with their husbands out of habit or duty, not because they still love them. Sometimes, when being "in love" ends, a stronger love grows and lasts. More often it doesn't. But people who love their work love it all their lives. I remember Lauren Bacall saying, "People should teach their children that work is what life is about", or words to that effect. She was right. The happiest people I know are those who adore their work, or have a consuming hobby.'

As she spoke, she thought of her aunt who had sacrificed her talent for painting to bring up nine children, care for an invalid mother-in-law and be a good wife to Ben. *She* had never expressed regret for the life which she might have had, but for her early marriage.

But Aunt Jo was intensely maternal and Alex knew that she wasn't—or had always thought that she wasn't. Yet now, as she looked at Laurier, savagely stabbing at his salad on the other side of the table, she felt a sharp sense of loss for the children they might have had together.

Dark-eyed water-babies, growing up in the sun and learning to swim before they could walk properly. Long-legged children being taught to surf by their father while their mother worked in her cool, airy studio overlooking the blue Pacific. In a matter of seconds a detailed vision of the future which Laurier was offering her flashed across her mind's eye, infinitely inviting, irresistibly tempting.

If he had looked up at her then, had reached for her hand, had told her how much he loved her, she would have been swept away, lost to all common sense.

But he didn't. He went on eating, his eyebrows contracted into a scowling black bar across his forehead and his whole face set in harsh lines, so that she had time to think, but that is just wishful thinking. Real life is never perfect. There are always problems and difficulties, and most of them would fall on me because the brunt of family life always does bear more heavily on wives than on husbands.

A man thinks he's doing his share if he runs the children to school, loads the car after a supermarket stock-up, cooks the occasional meal and takes his suits to be cleaned. All the rest: the grocery lists, the dinner parties, the thank-you letters after other people's parties, the organisation of household help; all that falls on the wife, and I haven't space in my life for myriad new obligations. I'm fully extended right now.

Too late, Laurier looked up.

'Work is important; I don't deny that,' he said. 'If you were, for example, a surgeon or a research scientist, someone whose work was important and had to be performed in a certain place, I could understand your attitude. Even if you were a singer or a soloist musician, then I could see your point. In that case you would have to travel; you would have problems meshing your career with your marriage. But being an interior designer is something else. It doesn't pose the same problems, or not from where I stand.'

'You mean from where you stand interior design isn't important?' she said flatly.

'I didn't say that. Do you rate your work as highly as a surgeon's?' he asked her, raising an eyebrow.

To stop herself answering rashly, Alex picked up her glass and drank from it, meeting his quizzical glance and realising, with a pang, that this was the very first time she had ever felt hostile towards him.

She was not a young girl who believed that love must be all of a piece, with few differences of opinion and never outright disagreement. But she hadn't expected *this* issue to be a contention between them.

She said, 'Actually I rate a dustman as being as important as a surgeon. Not everyone needs an operation but none of us could be comfortable without regular rubbish collections. As for interior designers, I think they're quite important in improving the quality of life. People's mental health is greatly affected by their surroundings.'

'I'm sure it is, but mainly in factories and offices, and public places. I doubt if the décor in expensive restaurants and hotels has much to contribute to mental health,' was Laurier's dry reply.

Still tired from the hours of anxiety during his absence last night, her nerves strung as taut as wires, Alex said in a low, goaded voice. 'Possibly not, but whatever the value of my work I wouldn't marry anyone who felt it was unimportant compared with *his* occupation. You wonder if *you've* been seeing straight.'

The strong hint of condescension in the way he had said 'If you were . . . someone whose work was important' had riled her more than he realised.

He said grimly, 'I'd have thought you'd been here long enough to know that Canada isn't a matriarchal society—and I'm certainly not in the market for a wife who's going to wear the trousers,' he added, with a snap.

'And I'm not in the market for a husband who wants to be a tin god,' she retorted, beginning to shake. 'Or any husband for that matter.'

Realising they were on the brink of an even more bitter exchange than the one in Victoria last night, and that—if it wasn't already—it would soon be obvious to other people that they were having a row, Alex took a tight grip on herself and went on, with frigid politeness, 'Please excuse me. I find I'm not hungry and I don't think there's any point in continuing this conversation.'

She put her napkin on the table, pushed back her chair and stood up.

It was a reflex action for Laurier to get to his feet when a woman who was with him stood up. The chivalrous manners drilled into him from childhood made it instinctive for him to half-rise now. But the realisation that she was about to walk out on him, her salad untouched and her glass of wine barely sipped, made the thunderous expression on his face comically at variance with the courteous movement of his body.

But Alex's strong sense of humour was temporarily out of

action. She was terrified of breaking down before she got out of the restaurant, and it took all her self-control to walk, not dash, to the door.

Once outside in the street, she almost gave way to her emotions but somehow managed to contain the shuddering sobs that welled up inside her chest. Blinking back tears, not seeing where she was going, she walked blindly away from O'Douls, with every step half-expecting to feel powerful hands on her shoulders and to be whirled round to face an even more punitive glare than the one she had turned from moments earlier.

But Laurier didn't come after her.

When she realised he wasn't going to, she had a terrible feeling they would never see each other again. In spite of the way they had parted, it filled her with desolation.

She knew that, although by coming to Vancouver she had upgraded her career, she had also ruined her life. She would never get over loving him.

CHAPTER FIVE

THE next morning Alex answered the telephone to hear the receptionist say, 'Mrs Tait is in the lobby, Miss Clifford.'

For an instant her heart leapt wildly. Then she realised he had said Mrs Tait. Could she have misheard?

'*Mrs* Tait? An elderly lady with white hair?'

'That's right, miss.'

'Please tell her I'll be right down.'

In the lift she wondered why Laurier's grandmother was calling on her. Perhaps Barbara Tait didn't know yet that their friendship had come to an end. He wasn't the type to confide his troubles, even to his much-loved grandparent.

As Alex stepped out of the lift, Barbara Tait rose from a chair near the desk. In the few moments it took them to reach each other, there was nothing in her manner to indicate that she knew something was amiss and that was the reason for her unexpected visit.

'Good morning, Alex. Have I chosen the worst possible moment to take you up on that invitation to see your designs? I should have called first, I know, but I had to come downtown this morning and having finished my errands I thought I would pop in and see if you could spare half an hour. But if you're too busy right now I'll go on my way.'

Foreseeing that it was going to be difficult to behave as if nothing had happened, Alex was tempted to claim that she was very busy that morning. But apart from the fact that she had always found it difficult to lie except to spare other people's feelings, she couldn't quite believe that Mrs Tait's visit was a spur-of-the-moment impulse. Women of her generation and upbringing were almost fanatically con-

siderate of the convenience of others. It seemed extremely
unlikely she would call out of the blue unless she had some
special reason for behaving uncharacteristically.

Alex said, 'I'm not too busy. In fact I was on the point of
taking a coffee break. Come up and see my eyrie.'

'What a delightful view of Coal Harbour,' said Mrs Tait,
when she saw the outlook from the suite. 'But don't you
think Coal Harbour is a most unattractive name for this
part of Burrard Inlet? The reason it's called that is because
one of Queen Victoria's survey ships, *HMS Plumper*, found a
seam of coal in this corner of the main harbour.
Unfortunately the name stuck.'

Alex stood beside her, looking towards the spinney of
pleasure boats' masts to be seen on either side of the
Bayshore Hotel.

She said, 'There must be a billion dollars' worth of yachts
and cruisers moored down there, and there are other
marinas crowded with boats in False Creek. But I've also
seen men scrabbling around in the big dustbins outside
hotels and apartments looking for something to eat. Most of
them, I know, are down-and-outs and alcoholics. But the
fact that the other day the *Province* reported the handing out
of eighteen hundred food bags to people in need does
indicate the extraordinary contrast in lifestyles in this city.
I've travelled fairly widely, but I've never been anywhere
where the chic parts of town and the sleazy ones are as
intermixed as they are here.'

'It's difficult for someone from Europe to realise how
young Vancouver is,' answered Mrs Tait. 'A hundred years
isn't long in the life of a city and, as you know, we didn't
celebrate our centennial until 1986. You wouldn't believe
how different Vancouver was when I was your age. Even
two decades back there was none of this highrise. Isn't that
an extraordinary building?' She was looking at the
Westcoast Building on Georgia, in the forefront of Alex's
view. 'I think it looks like a great foil-wrapped Christmas

package waiting to be lifted into the air by a giant helicopter.'

'I like buildings with glass curtain walls which reflect other buildings,' said Alex. 'John's architect explained the construction of that block to me. It's designed on the same principle as a suspension bridge. The floors are hung from those steel cables draped over the central core. It was built from the top floor downwards, instead of the usual way, and the lower floors were left out because they're harder to rent. It has greater earthquake resistance than a conventional building.

As she spoke a float plane appeared, was momentarily hidden behind the tall green glass wedge of the Crown Life office tower further down Georgia, and reappeared losing height preparatory to landing in the harbour. Now, every time she looked out of the window and saw a float plane, Alex felt a thrust of anguish.

'They say that, within your lifespan, the urban sprawl will have spread right down to the American border and all the way up to Hope at the head of the Fraser Valley,' said the older woman, a grimace expressing her reaction to the prospect.

Alex moved into the kitchen area to prepare the coffee. 'I've read that as recently as fifteen years ago there were hardly any restaurants here and only two theatres.'

'Yes, and now we have dozens of restaurants and a wide choice of cuisines, and a good selection of shows. But under the sophisticated surface, some small town attitudes linger on,' said Mrs Tait. 'Laurier never drinks when he's driving, but it infuriates him that somebody stranded at the airport here on a Sunday can't have a drink to relieve the boredom. By law it's still forbidden to drink in public places such as parks and beaches. Which means you shouldn't take beer on a picnic and you can't enjoy a glass of wine after shopping in Granville Island market.'

Her reference to her grandson had been made in a tone

of the utmost normality and she hadn't glanced at Alex as she mentioned him. Maybe she had no idea how things stood between them.

As she turned away from the window, Mrs Tait's attention was caught by the white cyclamen. Every few days Alex cut off those flowers whose delicate petals were beginning to brown at the edges. Today there were twenty flowers in bloom with many buds emerging from the thick foliage.

'What a beautiful plant,' her guest exclaimed, bending over it.

'Isn't it? Laurier gave it to me.' Alex strove to sound casual. 'I'm afraid I haven't any nice biscuits . . . cookies to offer you,' she added. 'I usually have an apple for elevenses.'

'I rarely eat between meals.' Mrs Tait glanced towards the models of the penthouse suits, at present hidden by dust covers. She didn't ask if she might take off the covers, but said, 'As you know, I'm on my own for a few days while Laurier is away on his hunting trip.'

Alex said nothing and Barbara Tait said no more until Alex brought the tray to the living area.

Then, as they both sat down, she said, 'I don't want to pry into what isn't my business, but I know my grandson pretty well and it's my impression he's gone off not to hunt but to be alone. If I'm right it can only be because something has happened between you which has upset him. You look rather down yourself. Am I presuming too much on a brief acquaintance if I ask you what has gone wrong? If I am, I won't press you, my dear.'

It was with mixed feelings of relief and reluctance that Alex answered, 'Laurier asked me to marry him and I refused him, Mrs Tait.'

An expression of surprise and disappointment showed on his grandmother's face. 'Oh dear, it's as bad as that. I had hoped it was just a tiff . . . something which would blow over. I guessed, of course, that he had fallen in love with you, and I'd hoped you returned his feelings. But you don't it seems?'

'Oh, but I do,' said Alex. 'That's why I'm looking "down". I've been awake most of the night, wishing I could marry him.'

'I don't understand. If you care for him, why can't you marry him?'

Alex wondered what hope she had of making Mrs Tait understand. Indeed in the long night watches, restlessly tossing and turning, her pillow often damp with tears, she herself had begun to feel it was an act of madness to have turned down Laurier's proposal and parted from him with the harsh words they had exchanged in O'Douls.

She began to explain the reason for her decision, a reason which, she felt sure, would elicit little sympathy from the other woman whose life, between finishing school in Europe and marriage, had been that of a 1930s débutante.

Mrs Tait heard her out in silence. This time her face didn't reveal what she was thinking.

After Alex stopped speaking there was a long pause during which they both sipped their coffee and Mrs Tait looked intently at the white cyclamen although in the manner of someone whose mind is not on the object they are scrutinising.

Suddenly she said, 'Has Laurier told you about his parents . . . his childhood?'

'Not a great deal. I know his mother came from Quebec and that he was born in Paris.'

'He was born there because Catherine—my first daughter-in-law—was studying music there. She and Robert, my son, were living in Europe at that time. Catherine felt herself to be a European. She didn't like Canada. She said there was no culture here and, in those days, perhaps she had a point. When Laurier was a little boy the cultural scene wasn't as rich as it is now,' Mrs Tait conceded.

'As soon as he was born she handed him over to a nurse and devoted herself to her career,' she went on. 'Everything was sacrificed to her ambition to be a great pianist. She almost ruined Robert's life. He was crazy about her, and I use the word crazy advisedly. He was besotted to the extent of giving up everything he liked to accommodate her desires. She wouldn't live in Vancouver. He agreed to give up his place as my husband's successor and become her manager. The five years they spent together were a terrible period in our lives. My husband was enraged by Catherine's selfish ambition and deeply distressed by what he saw as Robert's betrayal of his heritage.'

'What did they live on?' Alex asked.

'Robert had inherited some money and Catherine had a generous allowance from her father. She had relations in Paris who helped them to find a place to live. They had no financial problems. But he wasn't at home over there. He didn't pick up French quickly and he wasn't at ease among musicians and artists. It was a disastrous arrangement. I went to see them when Laurier was a year old. My husband refused to come with me. Although Robert was still in love with her, I could tell he wasn't happy.'

She had been looking out of the window as she spoke, but now she turned her face to Alex. 'That impression wasn't wishful thinking on the part of a possessive mother. I wanted Robert to be happy with her, although I was sad that his marriage had destroyed my husband's peace of mind about the future of the business. The following year I went to stay with them again. I thought then that Robert was drinking too much. By the time of my third visit it was obvious, although he denied it, that he had a drinking problem.'

'Were he and his father still estranged?'

'Unhappily, yes. But although he wouldn't have anything to do with Robert, my husband never objected to my writing to him, or visiting him. It's not a period of my life that I care to remember. I wouldn't be telling you about it, Alex, except to help you understand Laurier's background and the circumstances which shaped his character.'

'How terribly worrying for you. What was Catherine's attitude to her husband's drinking?'

'She was concerned but she refused to admit that the cure was to let him come back where he belonged. She wouldn't give an inch. I did begin to dislike her then. I could *not* understand how, loving him as she claimed to, she could go on rating her career as of greater importance than his health and well-being.'

'Was her career going well?'

'Yes. She was getting excellent notices for her recitals. Not only was she a gifted pianist but she was lovely to look at. Laurier's dark colouring comes from her. For the rest— his height and his craggy bone structure—he takes after my husband's father.'

After a pause, she continued, 'I'm sure it must help a woman pianist if she pleases the eye as well as the ear. Catherine had a beautiful neck and arms and long black hair which she wore held back from her temples by two combs but otherwise loose, flowing down her back. It was a delight to watch her play—but I couldn't enjoy it any more when I saw how my son was deteriorating.'

She fell silent, looking at Alex as if she expected some comment.

It seemed to Alex that Catherine had not been responsible for Robert's deterioration. If his only recourse in a difficult situation had been to turn to the bottle he was to blame, not his wife. But she couldn't say that to his mother. Instead she said, 'What happened in the end?'

'My husband had a heart attack. I cabled Robert and he flew home at once. As soon as he was back in Vancouver he seemed to come to his senses. When, several months later after my husband's recovery, he returned to Paris it was only to discuss a divorce. Catherine's family were Catholics but she had lapsed. She agreed to end their marriage on condition they had joint custody of Laurier. It meant that he had a very disrupted childhood, but it doesn't seem to have harmed him. It *has* made him determined not to repeat his father's mistake.'

'His father married again. Did Catherine?'

'No, she had a long-term relationship with another musician. In those days living together was much less common than now. My husband had old-fashioned views. He thought it immoral and that Robert should have sole custody. I really didn't care what Catherine did. I was just so relieved to see my son saved from alcoholism and married to a girl whose only concern was to be a good wife to him. That's another old-fashioned view; that being a wife and mother is an honorable profession which requires total commitment.'

'It isn't economically possible for most wives to stay home these days,' said Alex. 'One income isn't enough to support a family any more.'

'Maybe not on the lower income levels, but Laurier has some private means as well as his professional income. He could support a wife and children very comfortably. My dear, have you looked ahead to the middle years of your life? I know it's difficult when you're still in your twenties to visualise being thirty-five or forty-five or even—unimaginable!—fifty-five. But those birthdays come along surprisingly fast. A husband who loves you won't mind the change age brings. To him you will always be beautiful. Are you sure you can live your life without the security and comfort of a happy marriage?'

Alex hesitated, choosing her words. 'There's only one thing I'm sure about, Mrs Tait. That I can't live my life without the challenges and the satisfactions of my work. It's ... unfortunate that Laurier and I have careers which conflict, but that's the way it is. I can't function effectively from an island two and a half thousand miles out in the

Central Pacific. I could find some work there, I expect, but I don't want to limit myself to designing the interiors of holiday apartments and retirement condominiums. It's like asking Laurier to move to the middle of the prairies. He couldn't do what he does in Saskatchewan.'

She saw that Barbara Tait was not convinced. Perhaps it was impossible for someone of her generation ever to regard a woman's ambitions as being as important as a man's.

'The fact is that Laurier and I are as incompatible as his father and mother,' she went on. 'And, as they found, if one partner in a marriage gives up too much, it doesn't work out. Especially not with two people who are fully mature as we are. I'm not a young, malleable girl. My character's fully developed and I know that, however beautiful it is in Hawaii, I shouldn't be happy there.'

'Don't you think you should go there before you make up your mind?' the older woman suggested. 'You might fall in love with the islands.'

'I'm sure they're delightful—for holidays. But to be absolutely honest with you, even Vancouver is beginning to seem rather far from the centre of things. It's a delightful city and I've loved being here, but it isn't like London or New York or Paris. This is really an outdoor person's place. I'm a very cerebral person. I enjoy doing some outdoor things some of the time, but I'm not one of those people who long to "get away from it all". I want to be part of it all, right in the middle of it, where the creative action is.' She paused. 'It's hard to explain. I don't expect you to understand.'

'No, I must admit I don't,' said Barbara Tait. 'To me, nothing could be more important than a happy marriage. As soon as I met you I felt you were the right girl for my grandson. As his grandmother, naturally I'm biased in his favour. But I'm not alone in regarding Laurier as a very special person. I don't know a kinder, more caring man and, in a husband, kindness is very important. Many otherwise eligible men are not kind.'

'I know he is special,' said Alex. 'You don't have to tell me all his good qualities.' One thing she knew which his grandmother didn't was what a marvellously sensitive, imaginative lover he was.

She wondered if Mrs Tait guessed they had been to bed together, and whether her acceptance of modern behaviour was approving or disapproving. Probably her attitude depended on the participants' intentions. Laurier's intentions had been honourable. If the weekend on the island went well, he had meant to ask Alex to marry him. It was she who had behaved badly. Would Mrs Tait still think her the right girl for him if she knew Alex had gone to the island with the sole intention of indulging her longing to make love with him?

'Well, if Laurier can't change your mind, I certainly can't,' said Mrs Tait. 'But perhaps his absence will make you realise more forcibly how much you will be giving up if you *don't* change your mind. It's the most important decision a woman ever has to make, my dear. Or a man, for that matter. Going through life with a close companion, whether in marriage or in some other form of partnership, is so much more rewarding than living alone. Even now, long after my husband's death, I still miss having someone to share the things that amuse me.'

For a moment her amethyst eyes were sad. Then she smiled and said briskly, 'Don't think me interfering. It's not my nature, I assure you. I've said my piece and won't mention the subject again. I really did want to see your designs. That wasn't just an excuse.'

Later, after Alex had showed her the miniaturised suites and Mrs Tait had taken a gratifying interest in every detail and was on the point of departure, she remembered she had brought two books which she thought Alex would enjoy.

One was the biography of Pauline Johnson, the poetess whose grave was among the trees in Stanley Park, and the other was a collection of her poems.

By the time Alex had escorted her visitor to the lobby and returned to the tenth floor, it was half past twelve. Having missed the Phil Donahue Show, which she had intended to watch, she picked up the volume of poetry and flicked over the pages until her eyes were arrested by the name Lost Lagoon, the name of the lake at the edge of the park.

Sitting down on the sofa and slipping off her shoes so that she could draw up her legs and sit with her feet tucked beside her, a favourite reading position since she was a little girl, she began the poem.

It is dusk on the Lost Lagoon,
And we two dreaming the dusk away,
Beneath the drift of a twilight grey,
Beneath the drowse of an ending day,
And the curve of a golden moon.

It is dark in the Lost Lagoon,
And gone are the depths of haunting blue,
The grouping gulls, and the old canoe,
The singing firs, and the dusk and—you,
And gone is the golden moon.

O! lure of the Lost Lagoon—
I dream to-night that my paddle blurs
The purple shade where the seaweed stirs,
I hear the call of the singing firs
In the hush of the golden moon.

The three verses could not be considered great poetry, thought Alex, yet she felt they were charged with sorrow and vain regrets.

While she was eating her light lunch, she dipped into the other book, the biography of Pauline Johnson,

whose Indian name was Tekahionwake. Born on a
Mohawk Indian reserve in Ontario in 1862, who had
been the daughter of a well-bred Englishwoman and the
head Chief of the Six Nations, a sophisticated, cultured
man very different from the pathetic figures Alex saw
slouching about Vancouver, scrounging for money to buy
liquor.

A photograph of Pauline Johnson showed her as a
striking woman with a great deal of her father's race in the
aquiline lines of her handsome, intelligent profile. She had
never married. But when she died in Vancouver in 1913,
she had been cremated wearing a locket containing a
photograph of an unknown man—perhaps the man who
had been her companion on Lost Lagoon.

After lunch, unable to work, she took the book to the
park and sat on a bench by the path which skirted Lost
Lagoon. Several ducks waddled out of the water, hoping
she would have a snack to share with them. Presently,
realising she hadn't, they returned to the lake and swam
away.

Alex attempted to read but it was an effort to
concentrate. After a while she gave up and just sat in the
sun, thinking.

She wondered where Laurier was and if he was still
angry with her. She wished she had a photograph of him,
but perhaps it would be better not to have any mementoes
of their brief autumn idyll, except for the mitts he had
bought her to keep her hands warm.

She thought about Pauline Johnson canoeing on this
stretch of water long ago when Vancouver was still a small
outpost of civilisation and the lake a quiet, private place
undisturbed by the drone of traffic from the highway and
the voices of children running along the path.

Pauline Johnson had been famous in her day, giving
public recitals of her poetry not only in Canada but in
Europe. But her gifts and her fame and her unusual half-

Indian beauty had not brought her lasting happiness. Now she was almost forgotten.

And however famous and successful I become, in a hundred years' time I shall be dead and forgotten, thought Alex. Although it was warm, she shivered.

Mrs Tait's warnings echoed in her mind. Have you looked ahead to the middle years of your life? Are you sure you can live your life without the security and comfort of a happy marriage?

Alex was not at all sure. Less and less sure with every passing hour.

That evening she forced herself to do the work she should have completed earlier. About ten o'clock the telephone rang. Her heart lurched. There was only one person who would call her as late as this. Longing to hear his voice, she snatched up the receiver.

'Hello?'

'Alex, I just flew in. Do you have anything on tomorrow that you can't cancel?'

'Oh ... John ... Hello. No, I don't think so. why?'

'I'm taking a day off and I'd like to have you share it with me. I have something I want to discuss with you. I'll pick you up at ten. OK?'

'Yes, fine. But what shall we be doing? How should I dress?'

'We'll be sightseeing ... a mystery tour,' he answered, with a laugh. 'See you tomorrow.' He rang off.

Early next morning she went for her usual walk—she had missed it the previous day—and, coming back from the gun, was haunted by the memory of her first sight of Laurier running, of seeing his face for the first time and their first conversation.

The instant she stopped making a conscious effort to exclude him from her thoughts, things he had said to her, ways he had kissed her and touched her slipped into her mind.

She wondered if the same thing was happening to him, and if, as she had, he had slept badly last night, tormented by desire. Before going to the island, she had persuaded herself that a few days' happiness with him would be enough to last her a lifetime. She hadn't bargained for him wanting to marry her, or for her own abandoned response to his lovemaking. He had tapped springs of sensuality she hadn't known existed in her, making nonsense of her previous belief that having a man in her life wasn't all that important to her.

She was ready and waiting in the lobby when, on the stroke of ten, a sleek black chauffeur-driven limousine glided into view. The blue-suited, peak-capped driver got out to open the rear door for John Kassinopolis, who would have entered the hotel had she not emerged to meet him.

'Good morning, Alex.' As he held out his hand, he looked approvingly at the clothes she had chosen; a blouson of very soft, supple beige kid worn over a beige cashmere pullover and a cream silk shirt.

With Laurier she would have opted for gabardine trousers, but for a day with John a plain well-cut skirt of fine wool herringbone tweed seemed more appropriate. A scarf of black and beige silk was knotted round her throat and a pair of expensive English walking shoes with a leather-trimmed canvas shoulder bag completed her classically casual outfit.

'Good morning. It looks as if we're going to have another perfect autumn day,' she said, returning his smile. 'Good morning'—this to the chauffeur.

The huge car had soft velvety dove-grey upholstery and thick-pile grey carpet. It had more leg-room for its passengers than any car she had driven in. There were even raised footrests.

'Have you seen the paper?' John asked, as he settled

himself on the other side of the broad centre armrest.

He handed her a copy of the *Globe and Mail* and took up
the *Wall Street Journal* which he had been reading on the
way to fetch her.

As it was always necessary to wash the ink off one's hands
after reading the Canadian paper—it was even worse than
The Times, her paper in London—she was glad she had a
pack of wet tissues in her bag. Before opening the
newspaper she noticed that beside her was a panel of
buttons which controlled the electrically-operated window,
the temperature inside the car and several radio stations.

This is the life, she thought, smiling to herself.

And yet, as they swept past a bus stop and the people
waiting looked with curiosity at the occupants of the
luxurious limousine, she knew that given the choice of
going somewhere by public transport with Laurier or by
this means with John, she would unhesitatingly choose the
first alternative.

'Are you curious to know where we're going?' he asked
her.

'Naturally.'

'I felt like a sea trip. There's no ferry direct from
Vancouver to Victoria. We have to drive to Tsawwassen
which is about forty minutes south of the city,' he told her.

Alex tried not to show her dismay. The determinedly
cheerful mood in which she had set out disintegrated at the
thought of returning to Victoria where she and Laurier had
spent their last hours of happiness together before the
distressing débâcle which had followed his proposal of
marriage.

There were already two queues of parked vehicles when
they arrived at the ferry terminal at the end of a long
causeway. However, the *Queen of Esquimalt's* car deck was
capable of accommodating a very large number of cars
and, arriving with perfect timing just as the queue started
to move, they were soon on board.

A few minutes after they had climbed from the car deck to the passenger deck and were standing by the port rails in as rather fresh breeze which made Alex glad of her windproof blouson, their driver appeared carrying two old-fashioned steamer chairs.

'Where would you like these set up, sir?'

John chose a sunny sheltered position amidships. 'I found out that the seating on deck was limited and not particularly comfortable so I brought my own,' he explained to her. 'There should be a couple of rugs, Benton,' he added, to the driver. 'In spite of the sun it may be too windy for comfort when we're on open water.'

'The rugs are in the boot, Mr Kassinopolis, I'll bring them up with the basket,' the man replied.

It wasn't long before he reappeared with two plaid wool rugs and a large hamper.

John insisted on arranging one of the rugs round her legs, although he didn't use the other to wrap round himself but put it over the back of his chair. He seemed oblivious of the sideways glances and open stares that his solicitous attention to her attracted.

Alex felt a little embarrassed at being cosseted as if she were a fragile creature whom the slightest puff of wind might chill. At the same time it was very nice to have a comfortable chair to sit on rather than a hard slatted bench or the top of a life-jacket locker, and to have her nylon-clad legs protected from draughts.

She remembered his wife's ill health. Perhaps it was during Mary Kassinopolis's last months that he'd learnt to provide these careful attentions. Or perhaps very rich men, when no special facilities were available, always brought their own.

It wasn't until the ferry was under way that he opened the hamper.

'Have you eaten this morning?' he asked her.

'Yes, I had my usual breakfast but I wouldn't refuse some more coffee or tea.'

'I ordered flasks of each. You can have whichever you prefer. Like you I had breakfast at the hotel, but sea air sharpens the appetite. I asked them to put up some sandwiches and also a bottle of champagne.'

'Isn't it a little early in the day for champagne?'

'Not at all. Have you never drunk mimosas at breakfast? They're a blend of champagne and orange juice, a great pick-me-up after a late night.'

'In England they're called Buck's Fizz.' She had a sudden clear vision of drinking champagne at the cottage after their first time in bed together . . . of Laurier's hand warm and gentle against her bare breast . . . of being lapped in total bliss.

The sight of them drinking champagne attracted even more covert and overt interest from the other passengers. Not because she was hungry but because she felt the need of some blotting paper for the heady wine which an insulated container had kept chilled, she nibbled a cold roast beef sandwich.

For the first half an hour the crossing was not particularly interesting. Then the ferry entered a narrow passage between two pine-wooded islands. The swirls on the surface of the water showed the strong currents there. Suddenly *Queen of Esquimalt's* siren gave a loud blast and soon afterwards another ferry came into view, heading in the direction of the mainland. From then on the rest of the crossing was among large and small islands, some inhabited, some too small to be habitable.

Mercifully the ferry's passage didn't pass the Taits' island. She couldn't have borne to see the cottage; even looking at the other islands was painful.

To cover her inward anguish, she said brightly, 'Have you ever fancied owning an island, John?'

'No, but if I did buy one it wouldn't be here. My

forefathers were fisherman like those guys.' He gestured towards two men fishing from a small boat. 'But not in waters as cold as around here. I'm told that if you were in this water without a wet suit, after around twenty minutes you'd start to become paralysed with cold. My island, if I ever own one, will be in the warm Caribbean or the Pacific.'

'What about the Mediterranean . . . Greece? Have you been there? In search of your roots?'

He shook his head. 'I'm North American, Alex. I don't feel any ties with Europe. This is my continent—the New World. I doubt I would ever have gotten where I am in the Old World. There aren't the same opportunities for a man to succeed over there.'

'I'm not sure I agree about that. Some men will succeed wherever they happen to be born, and the New World hasn't been a land of opportunity for everyone who came in search of a better life.'

'For anyone willing to work it was and still is,' he said positively.

'Not for the Chinese who helped to build the Canadian Pacific Railway and then weren't permitted to send for their families. It's taken them generations of hard work to establish equal rights,' she responded drily.

She realised he wasn't listening to what she was saying but was scrutinising her face with a slightly frowning expression.

Before she could ask the reason, he said, 'There's something different about you today. I noticed it as soon as we met.'

'I'm wearing different clothes.'

He shook his head. 'I don't think it's that. I don't know what it is . . . maybe my imagination.'

He paused, continuing to scan her features and the bell of shining-clean hair which framed them. Unexpectedly he added, 'You're beautiful as well as talented.'

'Thank you,' she said, rather startled.

Was it possible the raptures she had experienced in Laurier's arms had made some subtle change to her personality which John's shrewd eyes had detected?

She said, 'You said last night you had something to discuss with me. Can we talk about it now?'

'Later . . . maybe over lunch. We'll be docking in a few minutes. When I'm talking business I don't like to be interrupted.'

It sounded as if he were going to offer her another commission. This morning the mail from Europe had included a letter from her assistant in London enclosing pictures of the interior of Alex's own flat torn from the latest issue of British *Vogue*. The feature would stimulate interest in her decorative style and probably bring in enquiries from prospective clients.

She ought to feel on top of the world, but she didn't. Deep down she had never felt more miserable. She couldn't forget the quarrel at O'Douls. It overshadowed everything.

It was already past noon when they reached Victoria. John instructed the driver to drop them at the Empress Hotel and collect them at half past three.

'We'll stroll around town after lunch but there isn't too much to see here. It was for the ferry crossing and to show you this famous old hotel that I brought you over,' he told Alex, as they entered the building.

Thankful that he hadn't chosen to lunch at the Laurel Point Inn, Alex accompanied him on a tour of the hotel's public rooms.

'The Empress is resting on its laurels. It's had a distinguished guest list and I guess for anyone important visiting Victoria this would still be the place to stay,' said John, holding her lightly by the arm as they walked through an interior arcade of gift shops. 'But afternoon tea at the Empress no longer has the social cachet it did in the old days. Now most of the people in here are coach tourists and it doesn't have the same atmosphere. It needs to be completely refurbished by that great young British designer, Alexandra Clifford,' he added, smiling and giving her arm a slight friendly squeeze.

Alex smiled in response. After going about with Laurier for some weeks, it seemed strange to be with a man who was barely an inch taller than she. But she couldn't help noticing that, although John didn't attract as many interested feminine glances as the younger man, her companion today made quite a few women look at him with more than fleeting interest.

In the interval since their first meeting in Vancouver he had lost quite a lot of weight and now looked noticeably trimmer around the waist. His thick grey hair showed no sign of receding from his broad forehead and would probably now remain thick to the end of his life. For an older man he was extremely attractive, she realised, in detached assessment.

Knowing the well-oiled wheels on which his life ran, it didn't surprise her to find that one of the best tables in the restaurant had been reserved for them.

'Why don't we start with a dozen Golden Mantle oysters and then try the veal cutlets with glazed bananas and grapes in wine and Cointreau sauce? Does that sound good to you?' John asked, after studying the menu for a few minutes.

'It sounds delicious,' she agreed, forcing enthusiasm.

When the oysters arrived, arranged on a silver dish, garnished with lemon and parsley, she was reminded of the night she and Laurier had feasted on freshly caught shrimps which he had claimed were a stronger aphrodisiac than oysters.

Closing her mind to the painful memory of the rest of that conversation, she wondered if John had lost weight because there was now a woman in whom he was interested.

'Mm ... these are good—and low cal!' he said, after eating an oyster and drinking the juice from the shell. 'This whole lot is only eighty calories. Did you notice I've lost a few pounds?'

'Yes, I did. You look very fit.'

He nodded. 'And feel a lot better. I just had a medical check. My doctor says I'm in good shape. I don't smoke. I don't drink much hard liquor, although I like this stuff'— reaching for the Pouilly-Fuissé he had ordered to accompany the oysters. 'I don't feel a day over forty. I may look it but I don't feel it.'

Alex wondered when he would broach the matter he wanted to discuss. She ate four of the oysters to his eight. They had never been her favourite seafood but she did enjoy the dry white wine. An attentive waiter was keeping watch on their table to ensure their glasses were replenished as soon as it was necessary. Within seconds of John draining the juice from the last shell, their plates were removed and the silver dish whisked away.

She noticed the service they were getting was better than at some of the surrounding tables. Perhaps the staff knew who he was and hoped for a generous tip, although from her knowledge of John they would be unlikely to receive more than the customary amount. He wasn't a man who needed to make lavish gestures to bolster his ego, and he would expect to be well served.

'You're quiet today, Alex,' he said, as they waited for the next course. 'Not that you're ever a chatterbox, but you usually have more to say for yourself.'

'I'm agog to hear what you want to talk about,' she answered.

'Right; as soon as we have our cutlets I'll tell you,' he said, watching the waiter lift the cover from the serving dish to reveal the presentation of their main course.

As soon as they were alone, he said, 'I've decided what my organisation needs is someone to spend time visiting all the world's best hotels and observing the special touches which have made them the best. We also need an in-house designer to keep an eye on the décor throughout the chain and give it a distinctive style which, without being boringly uniform, has certain recognisable hallmarks which give our patrons the comfortable feeling of being in a home away from home. I believe one person can combine those two functions and I'd like that person to be you.'

Even before he went into details about the salary, the expense account, the pension plan, Alex knew it was a fabulous job which most designers would jump at.

'Naturally it would mean giving up your studio in London,' John continued. 'But you'd still have a lot of scope. There's more to a hotel than bedrooms. You'd be re-designing restaurants, lobbies, conference rooms, coffee-shops, offices, beauty parlours, saunas, bars ...' He completed the list with a gesture. 'I know you like commissions which take you overseas. This way you'd be able to see the world a lot faster than you anticipated.'

'It's tremendously tempting, John, but——'

'But not so tempting you're going to say yes right away?'

She felt he had thought she would and was slightly put out.

'Have you ever committed yourself to a new thing without thinking it over?'

He touched his napkin to his lips. 'No one ever offered me a deal as good as this. If they had, I wouldn't have hesitated. What don't you like? Giving up your own business? Don't tell me you're making as much as I'm offering to pay you.'

'No, I'm not—at the moment. But maybe I can, in the long term. And as part of your organisation I'd be working anonymously rather than making a name for myself.'

'Now that's where you're wrong,' he replied. 'I was so impressed by a series of ads which a British agency ran for CIGA hotels, featuring their concierges—hall porters as you call them—that I told my agency I wanted a similar campaign. Right now they're featuring my chefs and their specialities. Next year you could find your picture in all the glossies as Design Director for the Connaught Corporation. You can't afford to promote yourself in that way.'

'No, I can't,' she conceded. 'But I'd still like to think it over. To stop being self-employed and become an employee, even on excellent terms, is a major transition. I've been my own boss for several years.'

'You've had a free hand with the penthouse. I haven't interfered with your ideas too much, have I?'

'Not at all.'

'That's the way it would continue to be. I don't appoint executives unless I'm one hundred per cent confident they can handle the job.'

He continued to press her to make up her mind for the rest of the meal, but when they left the hotel to stroll along the harbour front, he dropped the subject and talked instead of how, long before anyone else, he had foreseen that Vancouver's downtown development would move east from the so-called Golden Triangle towards the area where, comparatively cheaply, he had bought the lots on which the Connaught Tower was now nearing structural completion.

When they returned to Vancouver he wanted to see how her contribution was progressing.

'The models are finished. With your approval, I'm ready to start phase two, which is ordering everything. Then I shan't be needed again until the suites are ready to be decorated, which your architect tells me should be in five weeks from now,' Alex said, while they were in the lift.

While John studied the finished models she made coffee. He was drinking it and he was enthusing over the completed realisations of her schemes for the luxurious suites when he accidentally spilt an almost full cup of coffee down himself.

Perhaps the edge of the spoon had slipped under the base

of the cup, making it unstable in the saucer. Whatever the cause of the mishap, the sudden douche of hot liquid down his side and thigh made him swear violently.

Alex acted instinctively. Grabbing him by the arm, she rushed him into the bathrom where she seized the hand shower and directed a strong jet of cold water at the area soaked by the coffee. That it drenched him and swamped the floor was less important than preventing a bad scald.

Sensibly, John lost no time in unzipping his trousers and letting them fall round his ankles for her to spray his bare leg. But in spite of her quick reaction, there were signs that those first few moments when the coffee-soaked cloth had clung to the skin like a near-boiling poultice had done some damage.

'I think what you need is that aerosol stuff they put on burns and scalds now. There's a chemist just down the street, I'll run out and get some for you. Meanwhile it might be a help to rub an ice cube over the skin. Don't worry about the water. I'll mop that up when I get back,' she told him.

It so happened there were several people waiting for attention at the prescriptions counter in the nearest pharmacy, and the errand took rather longer than she expected. Hurrying back, it occurred to her that, had she asked at the hotel desk, they might have been able to provide appropriate medication from a first-aid box.

When she got back to her apartment, she found John wearing the terry bathrobe provided by the hotel. It was too large for her but on the tight side for him, exposing a thickly furred chest.

'I've called the Four Seasons,' he told her. 'They'll get some dry clothes from my suite and have them sent round right away. I also called the desk here. The maid will be along in a minute to clean up the bathroom. There's no reason for you to do it.'

'How does your leg feel?' she asked.

'It's going to be fine. Don't worry about it.'

She gave him the anti-scald lotion. 'I won't if you put some of this on.'

They had dinner together. Not *à deux* but with six other people involved in the Vancouver project, at Le Pavillon, his hotel's elegant restaurant.

It was an enjoyable evening with a congenial group, although at first the three wives were slightly reserved with her. She couldn't be sure if this was because she was a foreigner, an unmarried careerist, or because they suspected she had a personal involvement with the man employing their husbands. Trying hard to establish a rapport with them, she thought they could have no idea how little her confident manner represented her innermost feelings of heartache and uncertainty.

At the end of the evening the senior architect and his wife dropped her off at the hotel. With relief Alex said goodnight and collected her key from the desk, hoping there might be a message with it.

There was no message. No one had called while she was out.

When she was ready for bed, but not ready to sleep, she made a pot of mint tea and sat by the windows, gazing across the harbour to the lights of North Vancouver, thinking about John's job offer.

It was a fantastic opportunity; she should have been over the moon. But the fact was that nothing could excite her— or only one thing. A call from Laurier to say he was back in town and regretting the way they had parted.

As long as they were at odds, nothing else mattered, nothing else seemed important. If John offered her twice the salary and a vice-presidency, it wouldn't make up for this empty feeling inside her, this perpetual aching sense of loss.

At least I should *try* it Laurier's way, she thought, sipping the fragrant tea. I should go to Hawaii and see for myself what it's like.

She was tempted to call the Tait house and ask his grandmother if she knew when he was coming back. Then it struck her that he might have come back today. If he were to answer the telephone it could be difficult if not impossible to explain what was in her heart. It would be better to go over there tomorrow morning. She could return the books Mrs Tait had lent her and the binoculars Laurier had lent her. If he were back, she would explain how John's offer had made her realise her career wasn't all-important to her. If he were not back, she would tell Barbara Tait.

Alex woke up the next morning with a strong intuition that Laurier was back in the city. Going for her walk, she half-expected to meet him on the sea wall. She was disappointed, but reminded herself that it had been she who had walked out of O'Douls. That being so, why should he make the first move towards reconciliation? Except that mature people weren't governed by pride in matters of importance.

A few days before, the trees along Bidwell Street had made her stop to admire the blaze of yellow leaves. Now, after a wet windy night, in which she had woken several times to hear rain on the panes and to feel the tall building being buffeted, the branches were almost bare and the leaves lay in soggy brown drifts. The long golden autumn was drawing to a close. Winter was in the offing.

In the bus to Shaughnessy she rehearsed various things to say if Laurier opened the door, his dark face forbiddingly cold when he saw who had called. However, it wasn't Laurier but his grandmother who answered the door.

'Alex!' She looked very surprised to see her.

'Good morning, Mrs Tait. I've brought back your books and Laurier's binoculars. I had a feeling he might be back from his trip.'

The older woman gave her a rather strange look. 'Come in,' she said.

She ushered Alex into the living-room and gestured for her to sit down.

'Would you like some coffee?' she asked.

Something in her manner made Alex begin to feel uneasy. 'No, thank you. . . not at the moment. Is anything wrong?'

Barbara Tait seated herself. Looking deeply troubled, she answered, 'Laurier got back late last night. I was reading in bed but he seemed disinclined to chat. We only exchanged a few words and then he went to his room. This morning he told me he was cutting short his vacation and going back to Hawaii.' She glanced at her watch. 'His flight took off half an hour ago. He wouldn't let me go to the airport with him. We said goodbye here.'

On hearing he was already airborne, Alex had drawn in her breath in a gasp of shock. She couldn't believe that, even though they had quarrelled, Laurier would leave Canada without calling her.

'Did he . . . did he mention me?' she asked, in a low shaken voice.

'I don't think he meant to do so but I asked him if he had been in touch with you,' said Mrs Tait.

When she didn't elaborate, Alex prompted, 'What did he say?'

'At first he looked very angry and I thought he was going to tell me to mind my own business,' said his grandmother. 'Then he said, no, he hadn't because you had already said all you had to say to each other. When I suggested you might have had second thoughts, he said so had he. He had realised that his desire to get married and start a family had made him mistake the nature of your relationship. You had not done that. You had recognised it for what it was— a passing affair with no future.'

Alex couldn't repress a small muffled moan of despair.

If only she had called him last night, or first thing this morning. Now what was to be done? He was on his way to Hawaii, so angry and bitter about their break-up that if she called him there he might bang down the receiver.

'I think I may also have allowed my liking for you and my wish to see Laurier settled to colour my judgement,' said Mrs Tait. 'What my grandson needs is a girl who will be happy to build her life around him and their children. You realised that all along. Now he sees it too, and so—with reluctance—do I. But I want you to know that, had it been possible, I should have enjoyed having you as my granddaughter-in-law.'

'Thank you,' said Alex hollowly.

The sudden draining away of the eager hope of a reunion with which she had arrived at the house left her feeling curiously weak. She could think of nothing to say and felt too shattered to move.

It was over. Laurier had gone.

But how, if he had really loved her, could he have given up so easily? It must be, as Mrs Tait had told her, that a few days apart had convinced him that what had drawn them together had been only lust, not love.

'I think, early as it is, we both need a glass of sherry,' said Mrs Tait, rising.

That almost made Alex laugh, although there was more hysteria than humour in the reaction. For the kind of shock she had just had, a stiff whisky would be more appropriate than a ladylike sherry.

'No, really . . . not for me, thank you. I must get back. I have quite a busy day. I just wanted to return these,' she said, taking the books and the binoculars from her tote bag.

Placing them on a low table, she straightened and moved towards the door.

Mrs Tait accompanied her through the hall in silence. At

the outer door of the lobby Alex paused and offered her hand.

'I doubt if we'll meet again. Thank you for all your kindness. Goodbye.'

'Goodbye, my dear. I'm so sorry. . .' Barbara Tait's voice tailed away.

Alex walked briskly down the short drive, but once out of sight of the house her footsteps slowed and her slim shoulders sagged forlornly. The quiet streets of rich men's houses in well-kept grounds were almost deserted at that hour. There was no one to see her lips tremble, her eyes fill with hot, hopeless tears as she walked, head down, deaf to the rustle of dead leaves strewing the pathway.

If anything were needed to prove to her that she couldn't live without Laurier, it was the profound desolation she felt as she walked through Shaughnessy, knowing that the man she loved was far out over the Pacific, flying out of her life for ever.

CHAPTER SIX

ALEX was surprised to find John pacing the hotel lobby when she got back.

'Where have you been?' he demanded, with a touch of sharpness.

'I had a personal matter to attend to this morning.'

'You should have left a number where I could reach you.'

'Yes, I should. I'm sorry, John,' she apologised. 'Has something important come up?'

'The models are being transferred this afternoon, right? And when that's done you're free to leave here until the next phase?'

Alex nodded. She was supervising the removal of the models to the architects' offices immediately after lunch.

'Yes, but I haven't arranged my flight back to Europe yet.'

'Good, because I want you to come on a trip with me. It will give you a taste of the kind of life you'll be living if you accept the position I offered you yesterday. And a short vacation will do you good. You're looking a little peaked, Alex. Not that this will be total vacation,' he added. 'I want you to do a report on one of the world's best hotels. I want to know everything about it from the design of the matchbooks to the kind of soap in the powder room.'

It sounded just what she needed to take her mind off her troubles until the first shock had worn off and she could apply rational thought to the question of whether to accept Laurier's decision that there was no future for them.

'Can you be packed and ready by seven in the morning?' he asked her.

'Yes, easily. Where are we going?'

'To Waikiki, so you'll need some cool summer clothes and a swimsuit. If you don't have any with you, you can buy what you need when we get there.'

Alex was momentarily stupefied, scarcely able to believe that she was being handed a second chance to grasp the happiness she had let slip through her fingers.

'Is something wrong?' John asked her. 'Look, don't get funny ideas. This trip is strictly on the level. I'll be staying at the Royal Hawaiian, on Waikiki Beach, and you'll be at the Kahala Hilton, the other side of Diamond Head. Maybe I should have said *business* trip because that's what it will be. You have my word on that.'

'I didn't think otherwise, John. I know you're not——' She left the statement unfinished, finding it hard to express what she wanted to say.

He had no hesitation in completing the sentence for her. 'Not a dirty old man? I hope not. I'm no saint but you can trust me not to step out of line. You're a nice girl, Alex. I know that.'

His words reminded her that, last time she had been to America, a best-selling book had been called *Nice Girls Do*.

She wondered how John would react if he knew she had spent most of Thanksgiving weekend in the arms of a Canadian. Would he still think her nice? Or would he, being quite a bit older, still apply the double standard of his youth when nice girls didn't, or only with men whom they intended to marry?

He said, 'I must get back. I have a meeting at the hotel in ten minutes.'

'Where is the car?' she asked, there being no sleek limousine parked within view.

'I walk short distances now. That's your good influence.' He smiled and patted her arm. 'See you tomorrow.'

A little more than twenty-four hours later they were saying goodbye to the first-class cabin stewardess after touching down at Honolulu International Airport.

A chauffeur-driven limousine was waiting for them when they had been through the brief immigration and customs formalities. Before setting the car in motion, the driver handed over a box which had been on the front passenger seat.

'Ah, yes—this is for you, Alex,' said John. He opened the box and took out a thick rope of pink and red flowers. 'You can't arrive in Hawaii for the first time without receiving a *lei*.' He lifted it over her head and arranged the garland round her neck. 'It's also the custom to say *Aloha* and to give the new arrival a kiss. I hope you have no objection to my completing the traditional welcome.' Leaning closer, he kissed her lightly on both cheeks.

A delicate fragrance rose from the thickly massed petals. 'It's beautiful. Thank you,' she said delightedly.

He settled himself against the comfortable upholstery.

'It's a pleasant custom which has been devalued by commercialism. The souvenir shops are full of tacky artificial *leis* and some of the real ones given with package holidays are made from as few flowers as possible. But the *leis* which Hawaiians give each other in greeting and farewell, and on special occasions, are works of art in their way.'

'Have you been here many times before?'

'I have friends who own a place here. Mary and I were their house guests two or three times. When she was ill they lent the place to us in their absence.'

Leaning forward to address the driver, he said, 'Don't take the freeway. We'd like to drive along Kalakaua Avenue.'

'Yes, sir.'

'Kalakaua is the main drag through Waikiki,' John explained to her. 'It will give you a glimpse of the famous beach.'

As the car skirted Honolulu and approached the cluster

of tall hotels and high-rise holiday apartments which was Waikiki, Alex had her first experience of a city where the streets were lined with palm trees and the people, inhabitants as well as tourists, wore casual resort clothes and moved at a more leisurely pace than in a northern metropolis such as Vancouver. There, winter was waiting in the wings. Here it was always summer.

Although she knew it was a million to one chance that she would see him—at this time of day he would be working, not strolling about in a tourist area—Alex couldn't help scanning the pavements for a tall, rangy, loose-striding figure.

Presently the wide boulevard opened out on one side, giving a view of a packed beach and beyond it the ocean with surfers riding low rollers.

'That's Diamond Head up ahead,' said John, drawing her attention to a steep hill which had come into view at the far end of the boulevard. 'It's an extinct volcano. On the other side of Diamond Head is the suburb of Kahala where my friends have their place and where you'll be staying.'

Alex thought 'suburb' a misnomer for the elegant residential area separated from the city by the ancient crater. Through gateways in tall thick hedges of hibiscus and plumbago she caught glimpses of beautiful gardens surrounding luxurious houses. A few joggers and one or two gardeners in shady straw hats were the only people to be seen.

As the car swept up to the entrance of the hotel he had chosen for her, John said, 'If you don't mind I won't come in with you. I have an appointment downtown. We'll have dinner together ... at my place. I'll pick you up at six-thirty.'

Alex had lunched and dined at expensive hotels, but she had never actually stayed at a *grand luxe* establishment before. From the moment she entered the Kahala Hilton it was obvious that this hotel was as luxurious as they came.

From the lobby where she registered, after being greeted by name by a smiling reception clerk, she could see through a large airy lounge where huge circular Chinese carpets formed islands of deep creamy pile on a floor of polished parquet. Magnificent driftglass chandeliers hung from the lofty ceiling. Side and centre tables supported gorgeous arrangements of tropical flowers.

In the other direction there were some enticing shop windows and immediately opposite the reception desk a curving staircase descended to a lower level past a wall of dark lava rock half hidden by sprays of exquisite pink and purple orchids.

But it was the view from the white-railed balcony outside her bedroom which made Alex gasp. Immediately below her was a large free-form pool from which, to her astonished delight, a dolphin suddenly surfaced. There were three of them, she realised, spotting the shapes of the others skimming along under the water.

Close by the dolphins' lagoon was a large oval swimming-pool surrounded by a sunbathing area where a number of people with varying degrees of suntan were stretched on loungers facing a crescent beach of pale golden sand lapped by calm translucent water.

Some way out, a line of white breakers marked the reef beyond which the ocean was deeper, its surface flecked by whitecaps because the heat of the morning was tempered by a fresh breeze which tossed the fronds of the tall palms fringing the beach and dappling the sunlit gardens around the hotel.

It wasn't the pool or the sea which made Alex impatient for her luggage to arrive, which it did very soon. She was not in a hurry to unpack but rather to be left undisturbed to make the telephone call which had been in her mind throughout the plane journey.

This time there were not many Taits listed in the telephone directory, and only one with the right initials.

She knew it was possible that Laurier didn't go home in the middle of the day. She might have to wait until evening to catch him.

With a wildly beating heart, she dialled his number. She was holding her breath and her free hand was plucking nervously at the hem of her skirt as she listened to his telephone ringing at the other end of the line.

It rang for some time. Just as she was about to replace the receiver, a familiar voice said. 'Hello?'

'Laurier ...' Her throat was so tight with tension she could hardly speak.

'Speaking. Who's that?'

'It's Alex.'

There was a pause. Then, in a different, much harsher tone, he said, 'What do you want?'

'To talk to you ... to see you. While you were——'

He interrupted her. 'We have nothing to talk about. It was fun while it lasted, it's over. Forget it.'

He sounded as if he were going to hang up on her.

'Wait ... please ... Don't ring off,' she begged. 'I'm not in Vancouver, I'm here in Hawaii ... in Oahu, I mean. I must see you, Laurier.'

'You're here?' he sounded incredulous.

'I flew in less than an hour ago.'

'Where are you? At the airport?' His tone sounded more like his normal one. There might even be a hint of pleasure mingling with the astonishment.

'No, I'm at an hotel. The Kahala Hilton. Is it far from where you are?'

'Is Kassinopolis here as well?'

'Yes, he is, but——'

Before she could finish he cut in abruptly, 'Then you didn't come here expressly to see me, did you? And to put it plainly, I don't want to see you. We have nothing more to say to each other.'

He rang off.

For some minutes Alex sat frozen by his brutal rebuff. Had she misheard the warmer note in his voice when he thought she had come for no other reason than to see him? Perhaps, if she hadn't admitted she was here under John's aegis, he might now be making arrangements to meet her somewhere. But how, faced with a direct question, could she have avoided the answer she had given?

Surely, oh surely, when he'd had time to think about it, he would relent and call her back? If he didn't she would have to go to wherever he lived. Perhaps it would have been better to have done that in the first place, she thought regretfully. It was easier to bang a phone down than to slam a door in someone's face. And however angry Laurier was, he was too innately well-mannered to perform the worst acts of rudeness.

He would never, she knew, strike a woman, no matter what the provocation. To speak as he had just now showed how badly she must have hurt him with her stupid, reckless rejection of his tender proposal of marriage.

Tears sprung to her eyes as she remembered the loving expression in his as he had said, *This weekend has proved to me that I want to spend the rest of my life with you.*

And she, without pausing to think, had turned him down flatly and finally.

No wonder, knowing as he did that it had been feminine ambition which had wrecked his parents' marriage and disrupted his childhood, he was in a black, bitter mood.

For an hour she sat by the telephone, waiting and praying for it to ring and, as each slow minute dragged by, debating taking a taxi to his address. But in the end she decided it was better to wait a while, to give him time to adjust to the fact that she was here on his island.

Eventually, as the luggage she had brought from England did include a bikini and a giant square of cotton to wear over it, she decided to go down and swim. A short time later, having taken the lift down to garden level, she was strolling over the bridge which spanned the dolphins' pool.

To wade into warm blue-green water was a marvellous sensation, especially after taking off from Vancouver through a low cloud-base from which heavy rain had been pouring. She could understand why Laurier preferred to live in this climate. Who wouldn't?

The thought of him was an ache which she tried to dispel by flinging herself into the sea and striking out for the raft moored in the centre of the bay. When she reached it, she climbed aboard and sat facing the shore, her legs dangling, studying the exterior of the hotel.

About twelve storeys high and topped by a structure of uprights and crossbeams, the main block wasn't, in her eyes, an outstanding piece of architecture. She preferred the garden suites surrounding one end of the dolphins' pool, but to have had all the rooms at that level would have taken more land and the high block had the advantage of wonderful views from its balconies.

What an idyllic place for a honeymoon, she thought. The ache inside her regenerated.

The afternoon taught her a lesson: that for someone with severe heartache there was nothing worse than being alone in romantic surroundings.

At four she watched the dolphins perform. Their lagoon was aerated by a salt-water waterfall. Later, back in her room, she found a folder giving details of all the ferns and trees in the hotel grounds. It was something to include in her report to John.

'Are you comfortable here? Do you like it?' he asked, when he came to collect her.

Alex nodded. 'It's a fabulous place.'

He looked pleased. 'It was built in the mid-sixties. Killingsworth, Brady and Associates of Long Beach, California were the architects. The interior was done by a New York designer, David Williams. Most of the celebrities who come to Oahu stay here. It's quiet. It has style. On the way to dinner I'll show you the Hyatt Regency, which is quite spectacular.'

'Are you planning to build an hotel here?' she asked in the car.

'No, Waikiki has enough hotels. The Kahala Hilton is small—only three hundred and seventy rooms. But the Hyatt has more than twelve hundred and the five hotels owned by Sheraton have almost four and a half thousand. There are around ten thousand luxury-class rooms in this town and in my opinion that's too many.'

She was about to ask what, in that case, had brought him to Oahu when it struck her John might not want to discuss the nature of his business with the driver listening in.

Night fell early and swiftly in the islands, but in and around Waikiki the blaze of lights was even more spectacular than in Vancouver. The broad pavements of Kalakaua Avenue were thronged with strolling tourists enjoying the balmy Hawaiian night and the sight of moon-silvered surf rolling in from an unimaginable expanse of ocean to the south.

Further along, the avenue was built up on both sides, but before they reached that point John directed the driver to drop them off at the Hyatt Regency.

When the car pulled into the parking area, the door was opened for them by a dark-skinned doorman dressed in a pseudo-military uniform of white trousers, navy-blue tunic and white topi-style helmet topped with a swinging red plume.

As John turned to help her step out, the young doorman turned his smile on Alex. As their eyes met, she had an intuitive conviction that he was noting the disparity between her age and that of her companion and placing her in a category to which she didn't belong and disliked being included.

'This place cost a hundred million dollars. It's generally

considered one of the showplace hotels of America,' said John, as they entered the building.

Yet Alex preferred the hotel where he was staying, the old pink-washed Royal Hawaiian, its gardens lit by strings of pink Japanese lanterns, its corridors laid with thick sound-muffling raspberry-pink carpets. Sixty years old and now dwarfed by more modern buildings, Waikiki's 'pink palace' still possessed a special atmosphere.

'Although it no longer has a fountain flowing with pineapple juice,' John had said as he showed her round later.

They were seated in the restaurant and he was conferring with the wine waiter when three people appeared at the entrance and were greeted by the *maître d'hôtel*. At first all Alex's attention was focused on the beautiful woman and she didn't notice her companions.

The woman was partly Oriental. Her black hair and golden skin were enhanced by a simple dress the colour of apricots. With her was a man who also looked slightly Asian. As Alex glanced at the second man, her heart seemed to jerk to a halt. It was Laurier.

Led by the head waiter, the three of them came along the aisle which passed where Alex was sitting. Hypnotised by the compelling brown face of the man she loved, she waited for him to notice her. Perhaps he wouldn't. Perhaps he would pass without seeing her. In the circumstances it might be better if he did. What could she say to him in front of John and the others except stilted civilities which had nothing to do with what she wanted to tell him?

I love you. I've been a fool. Please forgive me. Forget everything I said to you at Laurel Point and at O'Douls. I've come to my senses. Oh, my love, won't you give me another chance?

Almost all the way to her table Laurier's eyes were turned towards the centre of the restaurant, his dark gaze ranging over the other diners as he moved with his graceful stride in the wake of his shorter companions.

But a moment or two before he passed John's chair, he looked to his right and saw Alex, her grey eyes wide with confusion and uncertainty.

She could tell he was as startled as she had been on first seeing him. But he had superb self-control. She knew she would have stopped dead had the situation been reversed. His pace didn't even falter. Something—fury?—blazed in his eyes as their glances locked. Then, without even nodding, he moved past, as if they were strangers.

'Is something wrong, Alex?' John asked.

He had made his choice from the wine list and now was looking at her.

'No, no ... nothing,' she answered quickly, forcing a smile.

To explain away the expression he must have seen on her face to cause him to ask that question, she made up the only excuse she could think of on the spur of the moment.

'I—I suddenly had a horrible feeling I'd left something important behind in Vancouver. But now I remember packing it, so that's all right.'

It was a meal she would never forget, although not because she enjoyed it. Her awareness of Laurier's presence, somewhere behind her, overrode every other sensastion. She hardly tasted the food and, by neglecting to drink her wine, made John ask if she didn't like it.

'You seem a little *distraite* this evening,' he said, after she had assured him she found it excellent.

'Do I? I don't know why I should be,' she answered untruthfully. 'Except that it is rather mind-blowing to be whisked from rainy Vancouver to this marvellous midsummer climate.'

'It may be raining here when you wake up tomorrow. There's often a breakfast-time shower at this time of year.'

For the first time since noticing Laurier, she was momentarily more aware of the grey-haired man sitting opposite her than the dark-haired man in another part of the restaurant.

'It must stir up some painful memories for you ... coming back to a place where you stayed with your wife,' she said gently.

'I can think about Mary without feeling pain now.' Kassinopolis answered. 'She wouldn't have wanted me to mourn her the rest of my life. In fact when she knew there was no hope of her getting well, she talked about the future, my future. She said that for me to marry again would be a tribute to her, a sign that we'd had a good marriage. Going to places we visited together doesn't make me sad now. But it does underline that I'm lonely without a woman in my life.'

'It shouldn't be too hard to find one. You're very eligible.'

'You mean because I've made money. That attracts the kind of woman I'm *not* looking for,' he said drily.

Alex felt they were now on terms which allowed her to speak fairly freely. 'I think you have much more to recommend you than your money,' she said, with a smile which this time was natural. 'And even nice women, who wouldn't dream of marrying *for* money, don't recoil from the prospect of being lapped in luxury if it happens to be part of the package.'

He laughed. 'I guess not.' After a pause, he went on, 'You once told me you'd never marry. Do you still feel that way?'

She didn't answer at once. Then she said slowly, 'No, that was a foolish thing to say, I've changed my mind since then. Now, if the right person asked me, I would marry and fit my work in somehow or other.'

Her insides clenched with the pain of remembering how the right person had asked her and she had refused him, turning his love into the fierce contempt she had glimpsed in his brief dark stare before, deliberately, he had cut her.

Was he watching her now? Or did he have his back to

her? She longed to look round but couldn't. John would notice, perhaps ask questions. Yet if Laurier were facing in her direction, watching her, and she never looked round, not once, wouldn't it seem like a hostile reaction to his cut? If only he knew how passionately she longed to heal the breach between them.

Forcing her mind back to John, she wondered if mentioning her work would cue him to press her for a decision about the job he had offered her.

Instead, dropping the subject they had been discussing, he began to talk about the islands which took their collective name from that of the largest one.

'As well as the four large islands—Hawaii, Maui, Oahu and Kuaui—there are about a hundred and twenty smaller islands which are the tips of a long range of undersea mountains,' he told her.

Inevitably this remark made her think about Laurier again. Presently she realised she hadn't taken in a word John was saying for some minutes. Fortunately he didn't seem to have spotted her inattention.

'A lot of Americans think Hawaii is in the South Pacific so a European can be forgiven for not knowing too much about the islands. Especially someone your age with no memory of World War Two.'

'You can't have been very old during that war, John.'

'Old enough to remember the catastrophe of Pearl Harbor. Now the Japanese are the backbone of Hawaiian tourism. Further proof—if any were needed—of the futility of wars. Yesterday's enemy is tomorrow's best customer.'

He summoned the waiter with a glance and asked for the bill.

A few minutes later, as she rose from the table, Alex did look for Laurier. He was quite close by, staring at her, his face an expressionless mask although she could see a tic at the angle of his taut jaw.

If eyes could convey messages, Alex had never tried harder to signal her unhappiness and her longing. His reaction was to turn to the other man and make some remark. Whether he looked at her again as she and John left the restaurant, she had no means of knowing.

The car which had brought them into town was summoned to take her back to the Kahala Hilton. As it swept to a standstill under the lofty portico of the Royal Hawaiian and a page sprang to open the door, John said, 'Are you tired? Would you mind if I drove back with you and had a nightcap at your place?'

'No, not at all,' she agreed, knowing how little likelihood there was of her getting to sleep for hours yet.

The last thing she wanted to do was to shut herself in her room and be tormented by doubts that she could make Laurier listen to her. Tonight he would probably stay out late with his friends. Tomorrow she would go to his house and force him to give her a hearing. She couldn't bear to believe that after the days and nights they had shared on a much smaller island, there was nothing left of the tenderly ardent lover behind the forbidding demeanour she had seen this evening.

Through the tall windows of the lobby the great driftglass chandeliers could be seen blazing with light as the car approached her hotel.

After telling the driver he would need him in about an hour, John said, 'How about a stroll along the beach?'

They made their way through the grounds to the moonlit crescent of sand. At the end of the beach a narrow spur of land, planted with palm trees, jutted into the still lagoon. A path wound along it and near the end was a bench.

'Shall we sit a while?' John suggested.

Alex sat down and gazed at the silvery foam on the reef. Overhead the palm fronds rustled in the warm night wind.

'This is certainly the most beautifully situated hotel I've

ever seen,' she remarked.

'Yes, this is one I should like to own. The operating company is a subsidiary of Trans World Corporation which——Alex, were you embarrassed having dinner with me tonight? Was that why you seemed uneasy?'

'No, of course not, John. Why should I have been embarrassed?' she asked in genuine astonishment at the suggestion.

Ought she to tell him the truth? she wondered. Before she could make up her mind, he said, 'I've always had a low opinion of men who chase after girls young enough to be their daughters. For a man my age or older to be seen with a girl in her twenties doesn't say much for either of them. What can they have in common? Usually he's only interested in her body and she's only interested in his money.'

He paused, evidently expecting her to make some comment on this statement.

'In general I think you're right, but I'm sure there are exceptions. A mutual passion for art or music might make a considerable age gap seem unimportant, don't you think?'

'I agree. There are always exceptions. I believe you and I are among them. I feel very comfortable in your company and I hope you feel the same way.'

Until a few seconds ago she had been comfortable with him. But now she felt vaguely uneasy. Where was this conversation leading?

'Yes, of course,' she said cautiously. 'But with my thirtieth birthday looming on the horizon, I don't see myself as a young girl.'

'You're still a lot younger than me. Twenty-five years. I'm on the wrong side of fifty. The natural partner for me is a woman in her forties. Except that a woman that age is past the best years for child-bearing, and I want to have children. My wife couldn't have them without endangering her life, it was a situation that distressed her more than it did me. As I've told you before, there was a long period when I was too taken up with business to have time for anything else. I regret that now. But perhaps it's still possible for me to experience the pleasures of parenthood. Will you marry me, Alex? Will you be the mother of my children?'

She was struck dumb.

The vague disquiet he had kindled by raising the subject of relationships between older men and younger women hadn't encompassed this astounding turn of events.

Floundering in total confusion, she stammered, 'I—I had no idea . . .'

'I realise that,' he said kindly. 'It's come as a shock. But don't dismiss it right away. Think it over, Alex. Take time and think it over—as I have.'

She didn't need time to think it over, only to find the right words for a gracious but firm refusal.

'I guess you've had a lot of proposals . . . a lot of guys in love with you,' he went on. 'I don't know why you turned them down but I'm glad you did. Many talented girls get married too soon and never fulfil their potential. Most young men are too selfish to make good husbands. I was myself. I expected to be the most important person in Mary's life, and I was. That was wrong. I was wrong to want that, and she was wrong to allow it.'

'She was probably perfectly satisfied to build her life around yours, John,' Alex murmured.

'Maybe, but it still wasn't right. If I had grown daughters I wouldn't want to see them involved in the kind of marriage I had. When it comes to the crunch, we are all alone in this world, Alex, and that's why it's very important for us not to be totally dependent on other people, not even husbands and wives. I realise now that if anything had happened to me Mary would have been lost. She had no strong interest in anything other than looking after me. She had no identity except as my wife. That can never happen to you. Believe me, I wouldn't expect you to give up your career. In fact I'm still hoping you're going to take the job I offered you.'

'John, I'm very flattered——' she began.

He moved closer and reached for her hands, taking them firmly in his.

'I should have led up to this gradually. That was my intention in bringing you to Hawaii. I thought if we had a few days together in a romantic setting you would begin to realise that my interest in you was no longer purely professional—or paternal. It hasn't been for some time. The day we went to Victoria I was sure we could make a very pleasant life together. What I haven't been able to guess was how you would react to the idea. Obviously it's come as a shock. You had no inkling what was in my mind?'

'No, none at all,' she replied. 'You've been at pains to make it clear that you weren't likely to proposition me, but I never dreamed you might propose marriage.'

'I don't know why not. You have all the qualifications to make a delightful wife. You're cheerful, intelligent, kind— the three most important things. And you're extremely attractive. More than that—beautiful.'

His fingers tightened. He leaned towards her. He was going to kiss her, she realised, swaying away to avoid it.

'John, listen . . . I'm terribly sorry but I can't marry you because . . . because I'm in love with someone else,' she finished, in a breathless rush.

He straightened, slowly releasing his hold on her hands. 'I see,' he said heavily.

'I would have told you before, if it had seemed relevant.'

He said, 'It's the tall, dark-haired guy who was in the restaurant, isn't it?'

'How did you know?' she exclaimed, in amazement. 'Surely I didn't give myself away to that extent?'

'No, you showed some reaction when he passed us. But I couldn't have guessed it from that. He gave more away than you did. Every time I glanced his way he was watching you or glowering at me. Would you mind telling me why, if you love him and he feels the same, you're not on speaking terms?'

'I don't know that he does feel the same—now,' said Alex.

Within minutes of John's proposal, she found herself telling him that Laurier had wanted to marry her, the reasons for her refusal and how their relationship had ended.

'But from what his grandmother told me, after he left Vancouver, I think he may have changed *his* mind as well,' she finished.

'Not if I'm any judge. That guy is being eaten alive by jealousy—of me,' said John. 'I'm pretty sure the reason he left Vancouver without saying goodbye is because he thought you were two-timing him. Not without reason,' he added.

'What do you mean?' she asked perplexedly.

'As soon as he turned around I recognised his face. The first time I saw him he was standing in the hallway outside your apartment. I was in my underpants and a bathrobe, you were down the street buying the stuff for my leg. The reason I went to the door when the buzzer went was because I thought you'd forgotten your key. He looked surprised to see me. Then he said something like, "I must have the room number wrong. Sorry to disturb you", and went back to the lift. I had no reason to disbelieve him. He was a lot more poker-faced that night than tonight. From what you've told me, I guess I was lucky not to get a sock on the jaw.'

Alex thought back to her last talk with Mrs Tait: *Laurier got back late last night. I was reading in bed but he seemed disinclined to chat.*

Unbeknown to his grandmother he must have returned to the city much earlier in the evening, gone straight to Alex's hotel, impatient to see her after their separation, and been confronted by John looking as if he had been in bed with her.

'But how could he believe that of me?' she murmured aloud.

'A guy in a bathrobe opening the door of a girl's flat is pretty damning evidence that they're on intimate terms,' John said drily. 'You can't blame him for thinking what he did. What would you have thought if you'd gone to his apartment and been greeted by a girl in a négligé?'

'I suppose you're right. And the fact that we've come to Hawaii together——Oh, God, now I'll never convince him it isn't true,' she said miserably.

'Maybe not—but I think I can. Tomorrow I'll go to see him and tell him what really happened. Then I'll tell him that I also wanted you to be my wife but you turned me down in favour of him,' he said quietly. 'Don't worry, my dear. He'll see reason. Now I think it's time we had that nightcap.'

When Alex went up to her room, she found a spray of orchids on her pillow. A fresh pineapple was another feature of the hotel's Hawaiian welcome.

Using a glass from the bathroom, she put the orchids in water and placed them on the night table. As she prepared for bed, she wondered if John would be able to convince Laurier of the innocence of their relationship. He had insisted on going to see him alone. There was nothing she could do but wait in suspense until one of them called her, some time tomorrow morning. If it were John who telephoned, she would know at once he had failed.

The bedroom was air-conditioned, with a refrigerator-bar and colour television. Perhaps later, unable to sleep, she would seek distraction by watching a late-night movie, if Hawaii was like mainland America where old movies were screened all night.

After fixing herself a long drink, she stepped from the

cool of the bedroom into the tropical night. The white-railed balcony curved outwards. Below was the large oval pool, all the sun-beds in orderly ranks ready for tomorrow.

Tomorrow . . . what would it bring? Joy or despair? The beginning of a lifetime of happiness, or the start of long years of loneliness and regret?

For a long time she sat on the balcony, trying to be grateful for the chance to stay in this beautiful place, but unable to keep her thoughts from reverting to the moment, a few hours earlier, when Laurier had stalked past her with a look of icy indifference.

It was long past midnight, and two hours later than that by her body-clock, when her telephone rang.

Who would call her at this hour? Not John. Certainly not Laurier, who thought she was here as John's mistress.

'Hello?'

'This is the desk, Miss Clifford. I'm sorry to disturb you but there's a gentleman down here who insists he must see you as a matter of urgency. His name is Mr Laurier Tait.'

Her silence made the clerk say, 'Are you there Miss Clifford?'

Alex recovered her voice. 'Yes, I am . . . Would you have him come up, please.'

'Yes, ma'am.'

Finding it hard to believe Laurier was actually here in the hotel and in a very few minutes would be tapping on her door, she rushed to the bathroom to pull a comb through her hair.

She was wearing a thin voile nightdress with rouleau shoulder-ties. The transparent folds showed the rosy areolae ringing the points of her breasts, her navel and the V-shaped outline of small tight curls. There was no part of her body which Laurier hadn't explored but that was then. This was now and she needed to cover herself with the nightdress's matching robe which was made of more opaque lawn.

When she opened the door to him, they stared at each other for a moment before he said, formally, 'It's good of you to see me at this hour. Did the receptionist's call wake you?'

Alex beckoned him in. She closed the door. 'I wasn't asleep,' she said, nervousness making her throaty. 'Or even in bed.'

With characteristic directness, he said, 'When I got back to my place, Kassinopolis's car was parked outside. He told me, among other things, that he's staying at the Royal Hawaiian and you're alone here. He said I'd completely misread the situation at your apartment the day I got back to Vancouver. He said if you married him you'd have a lot easier life than you would as my wife, but he couldn't convince you of that. Finally he told me to get over here and apologise—on my knees if necessary.'

He didn't smile as he added John's trenchant rider. His expression had never been more serious.

'I'm sorry, Alex,' he said quietly. 'I know it's a rotten attitude to have to admit to, but I guess for a while I found it easier to convince myself you had been to bed with him than to face the fact that you wouldn't shelve your career for me. I think I knew in my heart there had to be some good reason why he was there in a bathrobe.'

He took a slow step towards her. 'I haven't had a happy day or a decent night's sleep since we were together. That was a taste of heaven. Since then I've been in hell, knowing what it could have been like spending the rest of my life with you, and believing we had parted for good. Has it been the same for you?'

'Yes,' she admitted. 'Yes, it has. While you were away on your hunting trip, I changed my mind about work being the most important thing in my life. Since we broke up, I've realised it isn't. It *is* important ... very important. But it isn't as vital as love. If I hadn't spent those days on the island with you, I shouldn't have known what I was missing. But I did and I can't forget how wonderful they were,' she finished unsteadily, her eyes bright with tears of relief.

For a moment longer they looked at each other across the space between them. Then Laurier took two long strides and swept her into his arms.

He didn't kiss her. He held her tightly against him and she clung to him, her face buried against his broad shoulder as she struggled to control a tremendous upsurge of emotion. Very soon she found that she couldn't. It was too strong for her. All the battened-down misery and pain of the lonely days and nights since their parting welled up and threatened to choke her. Deep sobs racked her slender body. The tears brimmed and ran down her cheeks, damping his shirt.

'My love ... my love.' The huskiness of his voice betrayed how deeply her outburst of weeping affected him.

She felt his hand on her hair, his other hand stroking her back while he rocked her gently in his arms, murmuring words of love and reassurance but not trying to make her stop. He seemed to know that she needed to purge all the bottled-up heartache and despair of the time—and how long it seemed—since their last embrace.

The luxury of a shoulder to cry on was something she hadn't had since her parents were alive. There had never been anyone else with whom she could let her hair down as completely as this.

At last the outburst subsided.

'I need a tissue,' she muttered.

Laurier's hold on her slackened. A moment later he was tipping up her face and starting to blot her tears with something better than a tissue, a large clean linen handkerchief.

When she tried to take the handkerchief from him and to hang her head, he wouldn't let her, keeping her face tilted upwards, tenderly wiping her glistening cheeks and looking into her eyes with so much love in his own that her shaky protests faltered and died away.

'What was the matter with us both that we couldn't see straight before?' he said softly.

She gave a slight sideways shake of the head. 'I don't know. I must have been crazy to contemplate living without you.'

'We both were. I more than you because I've been around longer and I should be wiser,' he said, with a rueful grimace. 'I should never have asked you to maroon yourself in the Pacific. I know that now. Before I came back to Vancouver I'd worked out a compromise plan. If I can get myself a job at Woods Hole, you can make your base in New York. That would suit you, wouldn't it?'

'I don't understand. What would you do in Woods Hole? Where *is* Woods Hole?' Alex asked, her voice still uneven.

'Woods Hole Oceanographic Institution ... it's at the western end of Cape Cod. You know where that is, I'm sure.'

'Of course; it's the bit which sticks out like a hook from the coast of New England. But that's miles away from New York, and what would you do there?'

'Woods Hole is one of the four largest oceanographic research institutions in America. If I worked there we could spend a lot of time together. Maybe not every day and every night, but enough time to make the separations bearable. It's a solution. Not a perfect one, but the best I've come up with so far.'

'But I can't drag you away from Hawaii. You love it here ... the warm climate ... the sea ... the surfing.'

He drew her back into his arms. 'If you think that surfing can compare with making love to you, you underestimate yourself,' he said softly, before he kissed her.

She woke up in his arms.

The first morning of our life together, she thought,

nestling closer to him and lying in a happy daze until Laurier stirred and awoke and kissed her good morning.

Later they had breakfast on the balcony. If the floor waiter was aware the room had been booked for single occupancy, he was much too well-trained to give any sign of knowing that Miss Clifford's male companion was at present an unofficial guest.

'I think it might be a lot simpler to fly back to Vancouver to get married,' said Laurier, as they drank their orange juice. 'I checked out the formalities before our weekend at the island. I was sure we were going to come back in a hurry to organise the wedding.'

'Does our being of different nationalities complicate things?' asked Alex, thinking how virile he looked with a bath towel wrapped round his lower half and his bronzed chest gleaming in the sun.

'It seems not. All we have to do is apply for a licence at a District Register Office, wait two days and go ahead. A marriage commissioner can marry us anywhere: my grandmother's house, a hotel, even on a boat if we want.'

'Shouldn't you call your grandmother and tell her the good news? She seemed quite upset by our break-up.'

'I'll do that right after breakfast.'

But before they had finished breakfast there was an incoming call.

'I hope that isn't the manager wanting to know what I'm doing with a man in my room,' said Alex, rising to answer it.

'I don't think that's at all likely. If it is, refer him to me,' said Laurier, catching her hand and delaying her for a few moments to press a kiss against the inside of her elbow.

'Good morning, Alex. John here. How are things?'

'Things are wonderful . . . thanks to you. I shall never be able to tell you——'

'That's great. I'm delighted to hear it,' he cut in briskly. 'I've just had a call from LA and I'm flying there later this morning. Don't forget that you're still responsible for the penthouse suites, will you?'

'Of course not. John, I'm so sorry it hasn't worked out as *you* wanted.'

'Don't be sorry for me. Be happy. We'll keep in touch.'

He rang off without saying goodbye, leaving Alex to hope there had been no deeper feelings underlying his rather matter-of-fact proposal the night before.

'John has to fly to Los Angeles,' she told Laurier, as she rejoined him. 'Must you work today, darling? Couldn't we have just one day alone together in this heavenly place?'

'I think that could be arranged.'

He rose and slipped his arm round her. They stood by the railing, looking down at the tossing palms and the glittering sea with the shadowy outlines of corals showing in the aquamarine depths of the lagoon.

For a moment Alex remembered the lake in Vancouver called Lost Lagoon, and the gravestone among the trees, and the poem recalling a love that had somehow gone wrong.

Then Laurier turned her to him and took her face between his hands. As she closed her eyes and parted her lips for his kiss, she forgot Pauline Johnson and John Kassinopolis, and the problems of a modern marriage that she and Laurier would have to confront in the future.

Today all that mattered was that they were reunited.

ATTRACTIVE, SPACE SAVING BOOK RACK

Display your most prized novels on this handsome and sturdy book rack. The hand-rubbed walnut finish will blend into your library decor with quiet elegance, providing a practical organizer for your favorite hard-or soft-covered books.

Only $9.95

Approximately 16" x 8" when assembled

Assembles in seconds!

To order, rush your name, address and zip code, along with a check or money order for $10.70* ($9.95 plus 75¢ postage and handling) payable to *Harlequin Reader Service*:

Harlequin Reader Service
Book Rack Offer
901 Fuhrmann Blvd.
P.O. Box 1396
Buffalo, NY 14269-1396

Offer not available in Canada.

BKR-1A

*New York and Iowa residents add appropriate sales tax.

Can you keep a secret?

You can keep this one plus 4 free novels

Enter the world of Romance...
Harlequin Romance

Delight in the exotic yet innocent love stories of
Harlequin Romance.

Be whisked away to dazzling international capitals...or
quaint European villages.

Experience the joys of falling in love...for the first
time, the best time!

Six new titles every month for your reading enjoyment.
Available wherever paperbacks are sold.

Harlequin Presents

COMING NEXT MONTH

Available in July wherever paperback books are sold, or through
Harlequin Reader Service:

In the U.S.   In Canada
901 Fuhrmann Blvd.   P.O. Box 603
P.O. Box 1397   Fort Erie, Ontario
Buffalo, N.Y. 14240-1397   L2A 5X3

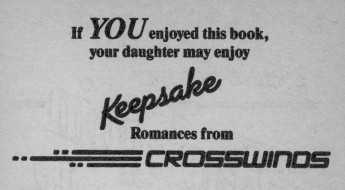

COMING THIS JULY

Harlequin Historicals

*Storytelling at its best
by some of your favorite authors such as*
Kristen James, Nora Roberts, Cassie Edwards

Strong, independent heroines
Heroes you'll fall in love with
Compelling love stories

History has never been so romantic.

Look for them in July wherever Harlequin Books are sold.